Emerald Isle

EMERALD ISLE

Maria Christine

A NOCTURNA PRESS BOOK

)3(

Emerald Isle
First Edition, 2020 Printing
Copyright © 2013 Maria Christine

Cover Design by Nocturna Press
Cover Photography: Auroras by Jamen Percy, Photos.com;
Eclipse by Silken Photography, Photos.com

Nocturna Press
Independence, Missouri
www.NocturnaPress.com

ISBN-13: 978-0-9854314-6-4 (paperback)
ISBN-13: 978-0-9854314-7-1 (e-book)

Library of Congress Control Number: 2015920694

Published in the United States of America

)4(

For the story lovers, and the story tellers...
Thanks for the inspiration.

CONTENTS

Chapter One

03₪

Returning Home

Miranda, an independent businesswoman, was in
dire need of an extended vacation. She left her
penthouse in the United States and travelled alone
to the picturesque and serene fishing village of
Kilcrohane, County Cork, Ireland.

It had been a long trip, yet a journey her
heart had ached for. The nearer she came, the
more she anticipated the road ahead and left her
anxieties behind.

As she approached her destination, Miranda
surveyed her surroundings; the lush green moors,
and the breathtaking view of Dunmanus Bay. Like

lovingly open arms, the mystical Ballyhoura Mountains seemed to graciously welcome her home.

It was dusk when Miranda arrived at the cottage. She hadn't been there since childhood. She stood at its door and breathed in the familiar vanilla scent of winter heliotrope and traces of primrose beginning to blossom. She felt renewed, at total peace, and she smiled from her soul for the first time in her recent memory. She was home.

The cottage was away from town, quiet, and charming. She cherished the memories of time spent there with her grandmother. She grinned happily as she traced the back of a chair with her fingertips and when she took the antique tea set from the hutch. She'd inherited the old cottage when her grandmother passed but had not been there since she was very young. The caretakers had kept the place just as she remembered. She knew she would have to return to the hustle and bustle of the city and her work at some point, but right now she forced it out of her mind. She was in Ireland to rejuvenate, to renew her senses, to relocate the magic she once felt in her heart. Somehow, she knew she would find it there.

Once night had fallen, Miranda took her tea and a quilt across the dirt road in front of the cottage and sat on the grass looking out at the sea. She was lost in the tranquility of her thoughts when someone spoke softly to her. "You don't see many primroses in these parts," said a dusky voice.

Miranda was startled half out of her mind and nearly dumped her tea. She turned to see a very tall gentleman standing in the moonlight. He was holding a covered basket that smelled delicious. "Who are you?" she blurted.

"My sincerest apologies, I didn't mean to startle you," he said. He silently held back a chuckle.

"Oh!" she replied, somewhat suddenly. "I'm sorry too. I didn't mean to jump. I suppose I was wrapped up in my own thoughts."

She struggled to stand up without tangling her feet in the blanket and he extended his hand to help. She took it right away and he pulled her upright.

"You didn't even spill your tea," he said.

"I guess I didn't," Miranda laughed.

Absentmindedly, she still held onto his hand. Now that she was closer, she could see his face more clearly. Even in the limited light she could see that this was an attractive man. He was very tall and powerful looking. He was younger than she expected, not too much older than she, and his smile seemed warm and generous. She felt her cheeks begin to blush and was thankful for the muted light. She quickly let go of his hand and secured both hands on her teacup.

"My name is Patrick. It's a pleasure meeting you," he said.

"Is that Patrick as in Saint Patrick?" she asked playfully.

"Not quite," he said. "I hope I haven't ruined your night, interrupting you like this." He broke his gaze and turned away slightly.

"Not at all," she insisted. "My name is Miranda. I was just out here enjoying the moonlight on the water and some primrose tea."

"Ah yes, the primroses," said Patrick. "Like I said, you don't often see them this far south, but Anna could always make them flourish."

Miranda was taken pleasantly aback. "You knew my grandmother?" she asked.

Now, Patrick was bemused. "Anna Kelly was your grandmother?" he asked.

"Yes, I spent the summers here when I was a child." She smiled at that memory. "This is her favorite tea."

"Oh," said Patrick. "Well, if that's her favorite tea, then I'd say it's got a splash of whiskey in it, eh?" he jested.

"A little bit more than a splash," she admitted.

The two laughed together for a few moments, but Patrick looked around and noticeably came to some realization. "I must be getting back home," he said. "I was just on my way there from town. But it was wonderful meeting the granddaughter of Miss Anna Kelly; absolutely wonderful."

"Do you have to go?" Miranda asked. "You're more than welcome to come inside for a spell." She grabbed the quilt and turned toward the cottage. To Miranda, Patrick seemed such a gentleman, and since he seemed to have known her grandmother well, she felt the least she could do was be hospitable.

"No, no. I can't," Patrick replied. "Thanks for asking. I'd really better go now."

"All right, if you're sure," said Miranda. "Will we see each other again?" she asked.

Patrick took her hand and kissed it gently as he stared into her eyes. "If I am truly that fortunate," he said.

His words unexpectedly surged through to her heart. His voice was like delicate thunder, the soft touch of his lips against her skin dazed her momentarily. He then slipped away into the darkness.

Chapter Two

ca๕ฆ

An Old Friend

Miranda woke the next morning to a bright and
beautiful day. She had a light breakfast of toast,
red currants, and a mug of tea. She was feeling
very revived this day. She'd spent merely one
night thus far, yet she already felt refreshed,
reawakened. She didn't even miss the usual iced
coffee and breakfast bagel she would typically
grab as she raced to work each day. She decided
to spend as much time outdoors as possible and
would begin by walking the grounds and
exploring the gardens.

It was mid-spring, and the grounds were very green. Touches of red, pink, and yellow had begun to appear. The blooms of winter heliotrope and primrose were already abundant. The back of Anna's property was uniquely full of trees which were tall and strong, and the branches were sprouting their leaves.

Miranda remembered fondly the days she'd spent in the gardens with her grandmother. It seemed to be Anna's favorite place. She would teach Miranda about the healing properties of the flowers and herbs, and how the energy from the trees could recharge you. She'd explained that all living things have a life force you can speak to, a spirit which could answer you back.

Miranda stared up at an old juniper and smiled wondering if it could hear her thoughts, when suddenly, someone called out to her. She was startled at the timing but turned around to find a somewhat familiar face. She was quite humored and relieved.

A white-haired elderly gentleman approached. "Well, if it isn't Miss Miranda Kelly!" he joyfully exclaimed. "I would know that mane of curls anywhere! Do you remember ol' Matt?" he asked.

Miranda was taken by surprise. "Matt? Matt Sullivan?" she recalled.

"That's me! Look at you all grown up. Your grandma would be so proud to see you now," said Matt.

Miranda smiled and hugged the kindly man. He had been a lifelong friend of her grandmother's and was always incredibly wise and gentle. "It's so nice to see you, Matt. It's been too many years."

"That it has," he said. "But you're here now. How long will you be stayin'?"

"I don't quite know," said Miranda. "I'm enjoying myself so much, I may not ever want to leave," she said.

"Ah, that's because you're home, my dear," said Matt. "Once the spirit of the Emerald Isle charms you home, it doesn't ever mean to let you go again," he said with a smile.

"Somehow I believe you, Matt," said Miranda.

The old man just beamed knowingly. "I'll bet you haven't seen any other folks yet," he said. "I just can't wait to tell them you're here."

"Actually, I've seen one person so far. A very nice man," Miranda explained.

"A fella?" he asked. "You'd best be lookin' out for them, girl. They'll be after a pretty young girl like you in a hurry. They'll pull all sorts of tricks," he teased.

"Oh, Matt," she laughed. "I promise he was an absolute gentleman."

Matt raised a brow. "Who was this gentleman? If you don't mind my askin'. I know all the folks around these parts."

Miranda thought back to the night before and smiled warmly inside when she remembered how he'd kissed her hand. "He said his name was Patrick," she replied.

"Patrick?" he repeated. He furrowed his brow and clicked his teeth as he thought of all the people who lived nearby. "I can't think of a Patrick close by. Where'd you say you met him?"

"Here. Well, I was across the road last night and he was walking by and–" Miranda stopped talking when she noticed Matt was staring blankly at her. His look was almost pained with concern. "Is everything all right, Matt?" she asked.

"Oh—Um, of course," he blurted. He tried to shake off his expression. "You know, you really shouldn't talk to strangers. And uh, you really shouldn't go out alone at night like that," said Matt.

Miranda only took him half seriously. "Why Matt, I'm a big girl. You don't have to worry," she said as she placed a hand on his shoulder.

"Patrick… nah," he mumbled under his breath. "Say, I'd better get going. But I might be checking on you from time to time."

"I would like that," Miranda replied.

Miranda spent much of the day outside. She was dismayed that she couldn't find the tiny red bridge her great-grandfather had built when Anna was a child and had placed in one of the gardens. She couldn't recall the exact location but thought surely it was still there somewhere.

Largely, her day was spent humming and picking flowers, and lying on the grass looking up at the clouds. Her days back home were always filled with noise, deadlines, and traffic. She wasn't used to relaxing, and honestly hadn't known whether she could handle it. But she found that she acclimated very quickly. She could get used to this life really fast, she thought.

When night had once again fallen, Miranda sat by the window of the cottage writing out a list of things for the market. The caretakers had stocked the cupboards pretty well, but she needed a few other things such as olive oil, pasta and brandy. And some herbs to plant since those were absent from any of the current gardens.

Suddenly, Miranda was overcome with the feeling that she was not alone. Her senses were heightened, and she looked out the window. She could see what appeared to be a man walking down the road. His only light was that of the moon. Somehow, she knew it was Patrick. She quickly stepped out the door to greet him. "Patrick? Is that you?" she asked.

The man stopped in his tracks and hesitated for a moment as she waved. "Why yes, Miss Kelly, it is."

Miranda smiled. "Well, come on over here," she insisted. "We're not strangers anymore."

He came to her as she stood under the porch light, and as he stepped into view, for the first time, he was fully illuminated. He stood close. She could see the rise and fall of his chest as he breathed. She was taken aback, breathless. He seemed even taller, more stalwartly built than in the dim light before. His eyes were the purest green and seemed to pour right into her soul. His hair was very short and brilliantly auburn, his lips looked as soft as they had felt when he had kissed her hand the night before. His face was distinguished, his look reserved.

"How are you this evening, Miss Kelly?" he asked. His gentle voice was deep and rumbled softly.

She felt flushed and placed her hand on her chest. She felt somewhat foolish for being her age and feeling the way that she did, and so soon after meeting him. She hadn't felt this way since she was a girl. She felt whimsical, almost giddy. "I'm very well, Patrick. Won't you come in?"

"Well, I was just heading—" he began.

She abruptly stopped him by taking his hand and pulling him inside. "Please stay," she said. "I mean, unless you have something you have to get to." She looked away suddenly thinking she'd been a bit too forward. After all, they'd only just met. She didn't want him to think she was a strange and desperate woman.

His lips curved into a very kindly grin. It was as if he knew her thoughts and wanted to make her feel more at ease. "I can stay a little while," he replied.

She looked up into his eyes and smiled.

Chapter Three

ᙡ

The Visit

Miranda was quite taken with Patrick. He was warm and gentle. They talked about the beautiful gardens her grandmother had nurtured and cherished, and he helped her complete the list of herbs to get for planting. She hadn't felt so joyful in years. He made her feel comforted, untroubled, even more-so than anything else had since she'd arrived. Their gazes locked onto each other's many times as they sat, but he would always look away first. She didn't notice this.

"This might be a silly question," said Miranda, "but you've spent time here with my grandmother… You don't by any chance remember a little red bridge?" She was sure he wouldn't know, but in the spirit of conversation she thought she would ask.

"Yes, I do," he replied. "It goes right over a narrow spring on the back end of the property. There's an old birch there," he said.

Miranda's face lit up. "Patrick, really?" She was quite surprised. "You don't know what it would mean to me to find it. It was one of my favorite places to play as a child. Would you mind coming tomorrow when it's light and showing me where it is?"

Miranda was truly excited, and Patrick didn't want to upset her, but he seemed unsure of something. "I, I won't be available tomorrow, I'm sorry," he said.

"Oh," she replied. "I understand. You have things to do. I don't mean to keep cutting into your plans," she said.

Patrick stood and took her by the hand. "But I can take you right now," he proposed.

Miranda was slightly flummoxed. "All that way at night?" she asked.

Patrick took the opportunity to kid her a bit. "It's a nice walk, unless you're afraid of the dark," he teased.

Her hand still in his, she took a step closer to him. Their bodies nearly touched as she looked up into his tender green eyes. For several moments they stared at each other, their breaths were becoming shallow; something between them was beginning to brew. "Patrick," she said softly, "With you by my side, I could never be afraid of anything."

She slipped slowly away, took her wool wrap from the hook and placed it around her shoulders. Unbeknownst to her, Patrick remained silent and still as she slipped out the door.

Chapter Four

 CR∞

The Little Red Bridge

Patrick led Miranda through the lush gardens and down a wooded path. Much of the area in Kilcrohane was open and clear, but Anna's land had a great many trees. Moonlight flickered through the branches above and lighted part of the way. It was peaceful, and for Miranda, it was somewhat exhilarating trekking through the dark woods with Patrick. She was unafraid, however. In fact, at that moment, there was no place on earth she would rather have been.

Miranda took each step carefully. She wondered aloud why she hadn't brought a flashlight or lantern, but Patrick didn't seem to need one. And roving through the woods by moonlight made her feel adventurous. It had been a very long time since Miranda Kelly had been on an adventure, possibly since the last time she was in these woods.

As they travelled, vague memories of the trail began to return to her. She was becoming more eager by the moment.

Suddenly, Patrick stopped and grabbed her by the arm. Miranda gasped.

"Watch your step," he said quietly. "There's a fallen branch." He then very gently helped Miranda step over the limb she could hardly see. Then he spoke again softly. "Do you hear it?"

"Hear what?" Miranda asked.

"The stream," Patrick answered. "It is narrow and calm, but you can hear it trickling along the rocks."

"Yes," Miranda said with a smile. "I can hear it." The sound was like a melody of perfect memories that played in her mind. She remembered it for the first time since she was a child. Her eyes became moist with tears of happiness.

Patrick took her hand gently and drew her a little further. There, near a towering birch, the moon's bright light shown down upon the little red bridge. The water flowed beneath it and sparkled brilliantly under the moon. Miranda was speechless, and Patrick knew wholeheartedly what it meant to her.

"Patrick…" she breathed as she knelt beside the bridge. She ran her hand along the rail. "The fairies have been using it," said Miranda.

Patrick raised a brow. "'The fairies'?"

"Oh yes," Miranda insisted. "It's worn from use," she kidded.

"Ah!" he replied as he sat on the ground by her side. "I can see that."

"You see," she continued. "When I was a girl, I would leave food here for the fairies. And when I would come back the next day, the food would be gone, so I knew they were real."

"Of course, it couldn't have been any of the other woodland creatures seen running about," he played along.

"Oh, no, it was fairies," she said. "I had a very vivid imagination."

Patrick looked up at the moon. "Sometimes you have to," he said.

Miranda turned to Patrick and stole a few moments to stare at the features of his face before his eyes turned to meet hers. They stared at each other in purposeful silence. Each meant to savor every second of this, lest they be few. Gingerly, Miranda broke the silence. "Patrick," she said tenderly. "Thank you for this."

Their faces neared each other's slowly. "I only led the way," he whispered as his eyes trailed slowly from her eyes to her lips. His breath began to quicken.

Miranda's heart began to race. She hadn't been this close to a man in countless months. She was too old to act on such impulse with a man she hardly knew. Or was she too young to know better? She couldn't remember. All she knew was that she wanted his kiss more than anything.

Her lips neared his. She could feel the warmth of his breath on her skin. She closed the distance and took his mouth into her own. She climbed to her knees and took his head into her hands. His hair was smooth, his tongue sweet and warm. Her body was beginning to writhe with hunger for him. He slid his hand up her back and pressed her closer to him. But then he stopped himself and broke from the kiss. She could see the tension in his eyes. He was fighting something back. "I have to get you home," he said shakily. "I'm so sorry… I have to get you home." He stood and carefully helped her up by the hand.

"I'm sorry, Patrick," said Miranda. She felt awkward, ashamed. "I'm so sorry. I shouldn't have assumed—"

"No, Miss Kelly," he interrupted. "You did nothing wrong, please believe me." His fingertips stroked her chin. "I am the one who is sorry. You don't know how much."

Patrick led Miranda back to the cottage, and she stopped at the door and turned to him. He could see her eyes asking questions he could not answer. He placed his hand delicately on her cheek and she closed her eyes and ardently received his loving touch. He apologized once more, before leaving into the night.

Chapter Five

ᘓ𝕎ᘔ

A Chat at Shivie's Pub

The following morning was bright and sunny. Miranda went shopping to fetch the items on her list. While she gathered herbs and fruit from the farmer's market, she thought of Patrick. He'd helped her compile the list. She'd hardly been able to get him off her mind since the night before.

He'd kissed her back, fervently, lovingly. But then he broke away. Why? He'd insisted she'd done nothing wrong, but he left. And she was sieved with a feeling of regret. Pushing him away was the very last thing she wanted to do.

As she held the sage to her nose and breathed its relaxing fragrance, she thought of him fondly. She hardly knew Patrick, but there was something special about him. He was a gentleman. He seemed honest and genuine, something she hadn't seen in many men. He was attractive in an infinite number of ways, his soothing voice, his deep green eyes. He was strong yet gentle; he was alluring, and sincerely benevolent. She desperately hoped she hadn't spurned any chance of seeing him again.

As Miranda put her groceries in the car, Matt approached. "Why hello there, Miss Miranda!" he said with a joyful smile.

"Hello, Matt! How are you?" she asked.

"Just fine, just fine," he declared. "Say, could you spare a few moments? I'd like to have a chat with you. Won't take but a smidgen of your time, I promise. I'll take you to Shivie's and buy you a nice oatmeal stout."

Miranda raised a reproving brow. "Isn't it a bit early for stout now, Matt?"

"Well, it's got oatmeal, hasn't it?" he reasoned.

"I don't think that counts," she playfully advised.

"Oh. Then how 'bout a raspberry fizzy, just the way you liked when you were a wee girl?" he asked.

"How could I refuse?" she said happily. She linked her arm onto his and was led to Shivie's Pub.

The two sat at a heavy round wooden table in the corner of the dimly lit room. Several older men about Matt's age sat nearby. They seemed to know him well, and all were dressed like seamen. The men paid close attention to Matt and Miranda, as if they knew of what they were going to speak. One of the men kept a lingering eye on Miranda as he sipped a foamy ale. She tried to disregard it as she listened to Matt intently.

"Miranda, I wanted to ask you about Patrick," said Matt.

Abruptly following the name Patrick, someone's mug slammed on the table silencing the place. Miranda instantly noticed.

Although he knew they'd be listening anyway, Matt lowered his voice and looked carefully into Miranda's eyes. "Are you sure that was his name, Miranda—very sure?" he asked.

Miranda took notice of the mood in the room and of the tone in Matt's voice and grinned charily. "Why?" she asked blatantly.

"Miranda, are you sure?" he repeated.

"Yes, yes! Why is it so important?" she asked.

"Oh, I don't mean to alarm you, girl, it's just that… ain't no one around here by that name." He feigned a grin.

"No one livin'," said the gruff looking man with the mug. The other men in the room began to whisper.

Matt's eyes shot over to the man and froze there as if he'd spoken too soon.

Miranda smirked as she looked back and forth between the two men. "Ah, yes… well, maybe I'd better be going," she said with wide suspicious eyes. These men must have been in the pub too long, she thought.

Before she could get up, Matt grabbed her hand to hold her. He then remarked jokingly, "Don't mind him, he's getting a little ahead of himself—"

"What does that mean?" Miranda questioned in a serious tone.

Matt couldn't seem to find the words, and Miranda was just about ready to get back to her herbs.

"Well, uh… What I mean is… there just hasn't been anybody around here named Patrick in a while…" he trolled off unfinished and the man with the mug spoke up.

"What he means is, the only Patrick around these parts is a dead man—a walking dead man." As his and Miranda's eyes were locked, he took another sip of his drink, never blinking.

Another man stood and noisily pushed back his chair. "Agh! You need your head examined, O'Malley!"

O'Malley, the man with the mug, looked partway over his shoulder toward the man and yelled back. "I tell you I've seen him myself! That man is dead, yet he walks these lands at night!" he slammed his hands on the table with frustration. "Just the other night I seen him back at the old lighthouse just as if he never was dead!" he shouted.

The other man threw his hands in the air. "Agh! If you've seen Patrick Hyland McShane workin' the lighthouse, you need your head examined!"

Miranda sucked in her lips and held back a laugh. She was quite humored but decided to grab her purse and attempt an escape. But first she looked at Matt whose head was in his hands as if things were not going according to plan. He raised his head and looked at her. "Look, girl, I know some of this sounds a bit hatstand, but you've got to hear everything…" he began.

She cut him off tenderly and with a gentle smile. "Matt, I don't know what's in those stouts, but the man I met is warm and gentle, and very much alive."

Matt's face was suddenly washed with realization. "You've seen him again, haven't you?" he asked as he watched her stand to leave.

She just looked away with her tongue in her cheek. Matt stood as well. "Miranda be careful," he pleaded.

She leaned in and gave him a kiss on the cheek. "Oh, Matt. You lay off the beer and you'll feel a lot better." She then turned for the door and called over her shoulder as she left the building, "Try a fizzy!"

Matt and O'Malley just stared at each other silently.

Chapter Six

ᨒᨘᨗ

The Lighthouse

Over the next few days, Miranda visited some of
the local sites, spent most evenings looking out at
the sea, and her afternoons gardening. She
planted all of the herb seedlings and thought of
how Patrick had helped her choose them. She was
enjoying her relaxing visit back home, but each
night that passed she felt she was missing
something. Rather, she was missing someone.

It was Patrick. He'd left that night and not
returned. With each passing day, her heart was
pained more by his absence. She felt more and
more that she had pushed him away, and she

regretted it deeply. Suddenly, this trip wasn't as enjoyable as it started out to be. And she was to blame.

The weekend had returned, and the night was dark as pitch. Miranda sat outside on the steps sipping a tea she'd made from dried primrose. She sat quietly and secretly hoped to see Patrick appear in the darkness as he had before. Then she began to recall her visit to Shivie's Pub, and the nonsense Matt and O'Malley were blathering about. As she sipped her tea, she chuckled to herself. "What a pair," she laughed. "What a pair."

But she remembered that O'Malley mentioned a lighthouse. *Patrick Hyland McShane*, she recalled. She played it over and over in her mind. That name was hard to forget. It rang in the ears and rolled off the tongue. It was a very nice name, whomever it belonged to. She wondered if it indeed belonged to her Patrick and if he simply lived or worked at this lighthouse they spoke of.

There was a lighthouse nearby, an old one she didn't think was in use any longer. She initially decided to check it out in the morning, but then pondered why she couldn't go that night. It was after all, a wonderful night for a stroll. Then she heard Patrick's sweet voice in her memory, 'unless you're afraid of the dark,' he had said before. This time, however, he wasn't there to escort her, but she certainly wasn't afraid of a little darkness. She cut a small bunch of primroses for him, grabbed her sweater and started down the road on foot.

Along the way, Miranda thought about all the ways she could apologize. She wanted to make amends with him somehow. Maybe she could make him dinner. She hoped he wasn't too insecure to accept flowers. Still, she knew she might not see him at all. Going by what O'Malley said was silly at best. Even if it was the same Patrick, what were the chances of her finding him at the lighthouse too?

As she came around the bend of the dirt road, she could see something tall beyond a few sparse trees. She knew it was the old lighthouse. She'd gone there once as a child but was told to stay away because of danger. Probably because it was an old building with steep rickety iron stairs.

As she approached the old stone structure it was dark and ominous. There were no lights anywhere. She could hear the ocean waves crashing against the bottom where the tide had come in. The iron stairs were gone. Instead, there was a small set of wooden stairs and dock surrounded the place. Miranda walked carefully around it looking for a window. She found one and peered in, the water sloshing on the rocks and sand not far beneath her feet. It was dark and the glass was dusty. Moonlight shined through another window and lighted a small area inside, but she could not see clearly for the dirt and algae on the glass. Suddenly, she heard and felt a hard step behind her. A hand flipped her around. She gasped.

"O'Malley! Matt! What are you two doing here?" she exclaimed. They'd scared her half out of her wits.

"We might ask you the same thing, missy!" Matt chided.

O'Malley was nervous. "Keep it down!" he whispered with great force. "He'll hear us!"

Miranda huffed and rolled her eyes. "Who will hear us? The wraith, Patrick Hyland McShane?" she deliberately blurted.

"Shh! Keep it down!" warned O'Malley. "And he ain't no wraith, little lady. He's some kind of living dead! That's much worse… much, much worse!"

Matt squeezed in between his fretful friend and an un-amused Miranda. "What are you doin' here, girl? It's dangerous out here at night. Can't you heed no warnin'?"

Miranda sighed. "I'll tell you, Matt, you almost sound convincing. But I think you two have been down here sipping a little too much cough medicine, and I should probably see you both home."

"You know, you ought not talk to your elders like that," said O'Malley. "'Specially since we was just looking out for ya'."

"Oh, really?" Miranda questioned with a suspicious grin. "How long were you two out here before I came?"

The men shared looks of guilt and said nothing.

Miranda laughed with tongue in cheek. "Ah yes, and were you drinking?"

"No, I tell you!" said Matt.

O'Malley looked at him blankly. "But what about the poteen?" he asked Matt.

Matt hit him on the shoulder. "Shut up, you!"

Miranda just laughed. "All right, let's just go," she said as she led them off the dock. She then followed the men to the truck they had parked in the trees and offered to drive. She looked up at the dark lighthouse one last time. "I didn't find what I came here for anyway," she sighed. She then laid the primroses on a large rock and jumped into the truck.

As they drove away, someone watched from the dark patch of trees nearby. His eyes glimmered in the darkness.

Chapter Seven

 confused

Please Come In

Miranda took O'Malley home first. He'd had quite a bit more of that homemade liquor than Matt, and by then Matt had sobered completely. He took Miranda back home and drove away, but not before pleading with her to listen with her ears and her mind and not with her heart. He warned her that the heart will lie to get what it wants.

Miranda cared a lot for the old man, and his words certainly were wise. But she knew he was simply superstitious, and he was letting his mind get the better of him. She wanted to remind him that the mind can also play tricks, but she held her tongue.

The midnight hour had arrived, and Miranda had just taken a long hot shower and was preparing to read a book. She wore a soft nightgown and robe and curled up in her bed. She tried to read by the light of the lamp at her bedside, but her mind was elsewhere. She thought of Patrick. She wished she knew his last name. She wished she could prove to Matt and O'Malley once and for all that he wasn't their mysterious Patrick Hyland McShane. But even more, she wished she'd been able to see him that night. She knew that Matt and O'Malley were wrong, thus, Patrick shouldn't even have been at the lighthouse.

Nevertheless, she was disappointed that she hadn't seen him. She thought about him more each passing day and was feeling tremendously ashamed for having moved on him so soon. She'd scared him away. How foolish she'd been.

She started to read what she hoped would be a tawdry romance novel. She never liked those kinds of books before. Typically, she read business magazines, or the scientific journals. Her whole life had become business, business,

business, and this trip was her chance to regroup, find herself again, and indulge in a little fun and fantasy.

She'd read a few pages when there was a light knock at the door. She was befuddled. Who would be at the door this time of night? Had Matt come back?

She slipped out of bed, tied her robe, and peeked out the window. Under the porch light she saw him. It was Patrick. She gasped and threw the book back to the bed, missing it completely. She wanted to hurry to the door but stopped at the mirror on the way. She still had a towel on her head—she flung the towel off and combed her hair quickly. There was no time for formal makeup, but that would have to be okay. In the middle of the night she wanted to look decent, but not overdone; that would be suspicious. She smeared on some lip gloss and speed-walked to the door. She took a deep cleansing breath and slowly opened it.

He was gone.

She ducked out immediately and saw him walking away. "Patrick!" she called.

He turned and came back. Her heart was filled with elation as the handsome man approached.

"I didn't want to bother you," he said politely. "I saw that your light was on and thought you might be awake. I can come another time."

"No! No!" she blurted, quicker than she wanted to. She reminded herself to be more reserved as not to frighten him away again.

He held in a chuckle as if he again knew what she was thinking.

"Please come in, Patrick," she said gingerly. "I've been so hoping to see you again."

His smile made her body melt with desire, but she tried desperately to hide it.

He came inside and stood before her in the dark with only the porch light to illuminate the room. She might have turned on a lamp, but reasonable thoughts seemed to elude her at the moment. The two simply stood frozen as if no time had passed since the night they kissed. They seemed still in that moment. As he stood before her, she suddenly had no thoughts of days gone by, of Matt or O'Malley, lighthouses, or wraiths or 'worse'… No, her ears and mind weren't listening at all, and if her heart was lying, it was doing a damned good job. He took her into his arms and kissed her, and she gave into him vehemently and completely.

Chapter Eight

❦

It's True

Patrick and Miranda's lips parted slowly. Neither could think of what to say. Their breaths were all that could be heard. Then, their mouths neared, and again they were locked in a kiss. Never before had Miranda shared a kiss like this, and she'd never felt what she was feeling for him. She longed for him, yearned for him, and now he was here. And he wanted her just as much.

She ushered him to the couch, never breaking the kiss. As he sat, she climbed onto him and he embraced her. She cupped his face with her hands and slowly slid her fingers into his hair.

His mouth was warm. His taste aroused her like nothing ever had. She began to moan, and a thunderous groan emanated from within him.

He suddenly broke the kiss, thrust her to the couch, and slithered over her like a lion stalking its prey. She gripped the front of his shirt and pulled him closer, and he ravished her soft creamy neck. Her chest heaved with desire; the weight of him began to press against her; and with every move he made, she ached for him more and more.

Patrick began to growl, almost like a beast.

"More, Patrick," she pleaded hungrily.

But instead he raised his head and stared down into her eyes.

"What is it, Patrick?" she begged.

His eyes were a richer green than usual in this subtle light, and his look was severe, almost foreboding. He seemed different, but she was unafraid.

"Patrick, what is it?" she pleaded. She was concerned for him. She knew something was wrong. She gently cupped his face once again and stared affectionately into his eyes. "Please, tell me," she whispered.

Patrick swallowed hard and his eyes washed over her delicate face. "I shouldn't be doing this. It's too dangerous."

"What is dangerous?" asked Miranda. "What do you mean? Please don't leave again." She could see that he was holding something back, maybe fighting something back, but she would not let him leave again, not this time. "You can tell me anything, Patrick. Tell me what's wrong."

Patrick looked at her almost in disbelief. She could see that he wanted to tell her something, but for some reason, couldn't. "You wouldn't understand," he admitted. He suddenly took a deep forceful breath, his eyes fixed on hers as if he'd said too much already, and he sat up.

She was still under him, lying on her back when she had a realization. And before she could stop herself, she asked him a question that he was obviously not expecting.

"Is your name Patrick Hyland McShane?" she asked, barely above a whisper. Her eyes were set on him, her heart was still. She was pinned beneath him and it was too late to retrieve her words.

His brow furrowed and he stared at her in disbelief. "Yes," he replied. "How did you know that?"

When Patrick questioned her, Miranda sunk a little further into the couch, but then managed to slide up onto her elbows and slither up to the sitting position. Her legs were still between his. He stared at her unmoved and did not flinch. Worried thoughts of O'Malley's stories flooded her head. She thought to herself that surely those tales were ridiculous… but still she couldn't open her mouth to speak another word.

Patrick bent down slowly and brought his face near hers. He searched her eyes for an answer, and, in a quiet baritone voice, he repeated himself. "How do you know my name, Miss Kelly?"

Her 'mind' warned her to tread lightly, but her hardnosed-businesswoman brashness began to resurface when he'd derided her with the words, 'Miss Kelly'. "Still so formal?" she asked spitefully.

She could feel the warmth of his body as he hovered over her, and she sat frozen as he slid his fingertips under her chin. "I don't like to play games," he cautioned. "Why haven't you answered my question?"

Miranda swallowed hard, but she knew she'd been evading his question and he had every right to be put off. She sighed and gave in. "It was my grandmother's old friend, Matt, and his buddy, O'Malley. They think that—" Miranda then closed her lips to keep from blurting out anything silly.

Patrick raised a brow and cocked his head to the side. "They think what?" he drawled.

Miranda squeezed out from under him and stood. She felt the slightest bit safer at a short distance and secretly sighed with relief. "Well… it's utterly ridiculous," she laughed. "It's not even worth mentioning really."

Patrick stood and took off his jacket. He wore a denim shirt tucked into his jeans. Enough buttons were undone to show his heaving chest. The look on his face couldn't have been more serious.

Miranda swallowed hard again and turned her back to him. "Really, it's just the ludicrous ramblings of two men who drink too much. You wouldn't be interested, Patrick." She then looked sharply over her shoulder toward him and corrected herself. "I mean… *Mr. McShane*."

Patrick sighed deeply and turned her around to face him. "Miranda," he breathed as he stroked her hair. "I need to know. Please..."

He already had a way with her. She would give unto him anything he asked. "Oh, Patrick." her look was now one of concern. "They say that you're supposed to be dead. They even insist that you're more than just a ghost, that 'it's much, much worse'. They tried to force me to stay away from you, but I couldn't. I can't! I don't know what's wrong with them." She reached up and touched his face. His skin had run cold.

He remained silent.

"Patrick, I know it's unbelievable! It's so preposterous that I—"

Patrick cut her off with two words. "It's true."

Miranda's brow weakened. She wasn't sure what Patrick meant. "What do you mean?" she asked wearily. She then, for the first time, realized how incredibly cold he'd become to the touch. She slid her hands down from his face and stood silently. She waited patiently for his response but didn't know what she expected him to say.

"It's true," he repeated. "I should be dead." He turned away and walked slowly to the door, closing it. He stood there for a time. Now the only light was that of the moonlight through the windowpanes.

"Do you mean you were in some type of accident?" Miranda asked.

"Yes…" he replied, "So to speak. Many years ago," he began slowly, "I was a sea captain."

It seemed to Miranda that Patrick was trying hard to recall his past, and he even seemed a bit surprised that he remembered, as if he hadn't spoken of it in a very long time. She also thought, however briefly, that he seemed young to have been a captain many years ago.

He continued warily. "I valued my work and enjoyed my life a great deal. But there came a time during the storm season when our village found itself in need of protection. The people chose the town's largest, strongest men to keep watch at night, and I was one of them. So instead of setting out to sea, I had a duty to stay and help my friends and neighbors. One of us would keep watch from the top of the lighthouse and the others would quietly patrol the grounds. We would trade shifts.

'One night, it was my shift in the lighthouse… and I saw what was coming. I ran down to warn the others but–" He breathed deeply, never lifting his eyes from the floor as he spoke. It was as if these memories pained him a great deal. "Something happened… and there's no way in hell I should be standing here now."

Miranda went to Patrick and gently placed her hand on his arm. "Patrick, I'm so sorry." He looked troubled and she didn't want to pry any further. She would not ask him for the details of his accident. She wouldn't invade his privacy anymore.

He turned to face her, and she could feel the warmth from him once again. She stepped closer until she stood against him.

"I should leave you, Miss Kelly," he breathed.

This time, she grinned at his formalness. "No, Mr. McShane, you shouldn't."

She slid her hand into his and pulled him slowly as she backed toward her bedroom. He was hesitant at first. She could see that his mind was talking to him too. It was telling him no, but she was hoping his heart—and body—would tell him otherwise.

He stopped firmly, and she had no other choice but to do what her heart begged for. She opened his shirt the rest of the way. She stared into his eyes as she did this, hoping he would let her continue. She then leaned in and softly pressed her lips against his smooth chest. She felt him breath in sharply when she did this. She then tasted him. She wetted his skin with the tip of her tongue, then gently sucked on his masculine curves. She felt his muscles contract.

She looked up into his eyes once more. "I want to be close to you, Patrick."

"Miranda…" he started to protest.

Miranda simply reached up and traced the outline of his face with her fingertips. "I want you, Patrick."

At long last, he lowered his head and took her mouth into his. Then he swept her into his arms and carried her into the bedroom.

When he lowered her to the bed, she slipped off her robe and removed his shirt. She could now see and feel his silky skin. He quickly removed her gown and laid her back gently. He took several moments to take in her voluptuous figure. He began to caress her curves adoringly. His every touch was gentle and deliberate. He was speaking to her soul with every delicate wisp of his fingertips. He wanted her as much as she wanted him, and possibly even more.

He climbed over her on the soft mattress and tasted her body tenderly. His mouth danced across her; his lips were like whispers that tantalized her waiting skin. She'd never felt this way before. Her desire for him increased with every passing breath. Inexorably, the two became lost for a time, absorbed only in each other's essence. All other matters drifted away. The love that they made carried them onto a transcendental plane where only love and ecstasy exist.

Chapter Nine

൭൹

The Accident

Miranda's eyes fluttered open. She felt satiated; all of her senses were renewed. She even felt a genuine longing for Patrick she'd never felt for any man. She thought to herself that she just might never leave Ireland. Her lips curved into a smile.

Miranda felt as if she'd slept for hours, but the room was still very dark. She turned to see if Patrick was still beside her, but he was not. He stood staring through the window, leaning on its rigid wooden frame. His arms were crossed, his silhouette was powerful, beguiling. He took her breath away.

Miranda sat up but remained quiet and watched him ardently. What was left of the setting moon shined just enough to enhance the curve of his strong jawline and muscular shoulders and to accentuate the vivid red in his hair. "You are so incredibly handsome," she breathed.

Patrick turned and looked charmingly into her eyes. Then he went to her. He pushed the blankets back and sat next to her on the bed. He stroked her hair back gently and kissed her as if for the last time.

Their lips parted but their mouths remained close. His hand held her head gently. "I have to go," he whispered.

She didn't want to hear it, but somehow knew it in advance. "When will I see you again?" she asked softly. She began to run her fingers through his silky-smooth hair and tried to subdue her coming urges.

"Miranda, there's so much you don't know about me…"

"I know all I need to right now," she insisted.

"No," he said as he turned slowly away. "I'm afraid you don't."

"Patrick, I really don't care about the past. It doesn't matter." She placed her hand on his back and caressed him. She tried to make him understand. She didn't care about the future or the past at this point. All she cared about was here and now.

Patrick stood. He seemed disturbed by something or upset. He dressed completely and stood at the window staring painfully into the night sky. Miranda wrapped herself in the sheet and hurried to him. "Patrick, if it matters that much to you, then tell me…" she said compassionately.

Patrick turned to Miranda and under the moonlight he looked straight into her eyes. His stare was piercing, deep. He'd been trying to tell her something but was unsure she'd been listening. "Miranda, I need to tell you about the accident that night. And I need you to listen, *really* listen."

"Of course, I will," she asserted. She stared at him now, with loving eyes.

"Miranda–I—" He spoke slowly and with purpose. It was, however, difficult for him to form the words he had never uttered to another living soul. "That night at the lighthouse… the night of the accident…"

"Yes…" said Miranda, her eyes urging him to continue.

Then, after tremendous effort, the words finally reached the tip of Patrick's tongue. "I lost my head," he breathed. He now stared at Miranda boldly and nervously awaited her response.

But Miranda's response was not at all what Patrick expected. She simply placed her hand on his cheek sweetly. "Oh, Patrick," she sighed with a smile. "We all lose our heads sometimes. You can't keep beating yourself up over it."

Patrick appeared slightly astonished. "Miranda," he said tenderly. "You don't understand."

"What don't I understand?" she asked tenderly.

He swallowed hard. He was taken aback by her unintended obliviousness. "Never mind," he said softly. "I want you to do something for me." He breathed deeply before continuing. "Promise me you'll do as I ask."

"Yes, Patrick, anything," she replied.

"I want you to get the gold medallion out of your grandmother's silver lock box, and I want you to wear it. Every single night."

Miranda was speechless. She didn't understand. Patrick kissed her on the forehead firmly then slipped away. Before she could find the words, he was gone. She stood at the window confused and stammered, "How? Why? *What lock box*?"

Chapter Ten

༺ༀ༻

Perception

The morning was dark and gray. The sun was
absent, and the air was cool. The town of
Kilcrohane had not been as silent in many years.
One could scarcely hear the crashing of the ocean
waves against the stony shore, and the wafts of
the gusting wind in the trees, but all other sounds
ceased. The birds and even the crickets could not
be heard, and the townspeople shut themselves
inside their homes and locked their doors.
Shopkeepers and pub owners closed early. They
were familiar with this silence, and although many

were too young to remember, they recalled the tales of what this air would bring.

One was never sure when the time would come. Days and sometimes weeks of terror, not knowing when he would strike—never knowing who his next victim would be but knowing that victims he would indubitably take. His charge was to sever the heads of those who crossed his path. His motives were fabled, but not a soul truly knew his reasons. And no one dared to stop him on the road and ask... for he was the headless horseman.

Miranda Kelly woke late that morning. Before she'd opened her eyes, she instinctively placed her hand where Patrick had laid. His absence woke her. It was then that she realized the new day had come and remembered that he had gone. Her night with him had been more than wonderful, it was almost supernatural. His affection with her was unparalleled; the passion he invoked in her was immeasurable. She felt awakened somehow, changed, and for the better.

Miranda sat outside in her cardigan sweater. Underneath it she wore her favorite t-shirt. It had a third eye in the center. She'd been floating on air since she'd arrived there, and while she was still high on the atmosphere, she was beginning to feel more like herself again. She was liberated and happy. Her auburn locks were swept up loosely. She sipped hot tea from her mug and enjoyed the chilly afternoon air. The last thing she remembered about the night before was Patrick's loving embrace. Apart from that, she didn't have a care in the world.

A familiar truck pulled up the dirt road and parked in front of the cottage. It was her good friend, Matt Sullivan.

"What brings you here, Matt?" she asked warmly as he exited the truck.

"Hello there, Miranda. I came to have a talk with you," he said.

"About the weather I hope," said Miranda. She smiled as she kidded, but she sincerely hoped he didn't want to talk about Patrick. She sipped her tea once more.

"I know you don't want to listen, Miranda," said Matt. "But this time I pray you will. It's not just about Patrick. There are things about this place that you just don't understand. And I think your grandma would want me to tell you everything I know."

Miranda agreed and led Matt inside.

Miranda listened to the distant rumble of thunder that warned of the coming storm as she poured hot tea for herself and for Matt. She watched as he stoked the logs in the burning fireplace.

Matt had been very close to her grandmother and Miranda always felt they cared for each other very deeply, possibly even loved each other. But so far as she knew, nothing more ever came of it, and she often wondered why not. He was a caring, generous man, and for the life of her, Miranda couldn't understand why he was so frenzied about Patrick Hyland McShane.

Matt saw Miranda with the tea tray, and both sat in the chairs by the fire.

"Miranda," Matt began. "I'm afraid you must think me a couple cans short of a picnic."

"Never," she replied honestly.

He looked doubtfully into her eyes and she sighed. "But you have been a little high-strung lately," she affirmed.

"Well, I think I'd better explain it without any further delay," he insisted. "We may not have much time."

Miranda set her tea aside for a moment, her brow lowered with worry. Matt spoke with such seriousness that she truly became concerned. "All right, Matt," said Miranda. "I'm listening."

"Miranda, forty-three years ago I was a young seaman. There were three of us who were thick as thieves. Oh, each of us fancied himself the greatest fisherman on all the sea, but truth be said, weren't three greater friends in the world." His head hung lower as he forced himself to continue.

"Then, evil came to our town. It was something so menacing, so dreadful—something we'd only heard tell of from the old folks when we were coming up. They even said it came when we was boys; but didn't none of us younger fellas want to believe it. Then one day the wind just changed. There was something different on the air. Something dark. The old folks knew what was comin'. They called for the strongest of the men to keep guard at night, mostly seamen, ploughmen. This was a couple years after they put up the new lighthouse down the way. We used this old one near here to keep lookout o'er the village. My two friends and I took shifts up there."

Miranda choked on her tea just then and her cup clinked against the saucer. She placed them down immediately and stared at Matt charily.

"What is it, Miranda?" Matt asked sharply.

"Oh, it's nothing," she replied. She stood and tried to gather herself as she walked to the window. She'd been caught off guard when Matt's story began to mirror the one Patrick had told. She'd forgotten Patrick's story until precisely that moment. "Please continue," she beseeched as she stared out into the darkening sky.

Matt stood as well. The thunder was closer. He stared at the young woman whose back was to him. "One of my friends was O'Malley," he said. "It was the dead of night. As you know, there's a little bit of woods just by the lighthouse. Not much, just a little. The two of us were tucked away in there nervously watching the road from the underbrush. That's when it happened."

Miranda turned to face him, her interest peaked, and now it was he who turned away. It was apparent he spoke these last words with great difficulty.

"It happened so fast." He swallowed hard. "There was nothing we could do. The hooves pummeled the ground like a herd of horses. And then all at once the black rider was upon us! We couldn't see nothin' but the whip of his cape and the rearing black beast he was riding. Its neigh was like the screams of burning souls! Then he came down to warn us. He came running from the lighthouse!"

Miranda's eyes were wide and fixed on the grief-stricken older man. He was still terrified after all these years. He'd turned to her and held tight to her shoulders, his eyes wet with the remembrance of terror and grief. Then, he was barely able to utter the mind-blowing words, "He didn't have a chance. The dullahan pointed his sword and called him by name. And then he did his worst. The whoosh of that sword on the wind is burned in my mind forever. Our Patrick never had a chance!"

Chapter Eleven

☙

Leave this Place

Miranda was stammered by Matt's story. Her mind was befuddled with thoughts and questions. Matt was very visibly shaken. His words rang true. But how could this be? How could his story be so similar to Patrick's? How could Patrick be that age? How could he still be alive? Nothing made sense. And yet it made too much sense. She closed her eyes as Matt still clutched her by the arms. She was overwhelmed. She felt faint.

"Miranda? Speak to me, girl," said Matt. He was worried the news had been too much.

Miranda opened her eyes, but she failed to speak. She gazed low into nothing. She broke from Matt and turned to the couch where she and Patrick had laid the night before. She knelt on the cushion and placed her hand where his had been when he was mounted over her asking how she knew his name. She tried to rationalize her thoughts but couldn't. She sat and took slow bated breaths. She decided the story was real, and therefore, the only thing in question was her lucidity.

"Miranda, are you all right?" Matt asked softly.

"I feel all right," she replied. "But my mind is telling me otherwise." She turned her head to the window and saw the rain beginning to fall.

"Now, Miranda, I don't want you thinkin' those thoughts," said Matt. "I know it's a lot to digest, but you can't go questioning your sanity. It's all true. I wish it weren't, but it is." He looked out at the storm and his voice became anxious. "Miranda, when is the last time you saw Patrick?"

She silently thought back to the night before. She remembered the feel of his hands and lips on her skin, the loving attention he paid her, his inebriating scent, his soulful gaze.

Matt stood a little straighter. He'd been afraid of this. She hadn't said a word, but he saw the look on her face and knew. She'd fallen in love with him. He could only cling to the faintest shred of hope that this was not the same man.

"Miranda… has he told you his full name?" he asked hesitantly.

She stood and faced the window once more. "Yes," she breathed.

"Is it—" he began.

"Yes," she replied.

Matt's heart sunk low. It was broken for his long-lost friend, but now for her as well. And the idea that Patrick was somehow back from the dead had plagued him, but now, knowing it was true shook him to the core. He was at a loss.

Suddenly, Matt recovered his senses and became exceedingly more alarmed than before. "Miranda!" he yelled. "There's something else I haven't told you! The dullahan—he's most assuredly on his way. There's a change in the air. I know it, the town knows it."

Miranda turned quickly. She was still attempting to rationalize everything in her head. Surely there must be some logical explanation. Her mind tried to work it out, but her heart told her it was pointless. She wondered which part of her was lying this time. "Matt, are you saying the headless horseman is on his way to Kilcrohane?"

"I'm tellin' you he's likely already here. And after hearing the last words I heard him speak after slashing my friend, I'm even more afraid for your safety."

Miranda was frightened by his tone. "What words?" she asked.

Matt took a deep breath. "He said, 'Patrick Hyland McShane, I'll be back for you'."

Pain and unease suddenly shot through Miranda's heart. Rationale left her for good. All at once she didn't care what was real or fantasy. She only cared for Patrick's well-being.

Matt saw her reaction to his words and was more terrified for her than ever. "You love him, don't you?" he asked knowingly.

"Love…" she whispered. She held her stomach tightly. She was overcome by her feelings.

Matt sighed with frustration and concern. "That's why you've got to leave this place, girl—tonight. If he's comin' after Patrick, then you are most certainly not safe!"

Chapter Twelve

⊂Ω∽

Primroses

"He'll be back for him?" Miranda questioned aloud. She disregarded Matt's warning; her eyes began to shift back and forth. She felt her shrewdness was waning. Her mind was a whirlwind of mixed emotions teetering one way and then the other, but as the seconds and minutes passed, she began to firmly believe.

Matt tried to regain her attention. "Look, girl, you've got to leave this place!" he reminded. "Didn't you hear what I said?"

He was anxious, but her mind was elsewhere. Then something suddenly clicked. Patrick had mentioned a silver lock box. If there truly was one, maybe it would hold some answers. "I'm not going anywhere, Matt. I've got to find that box." She took off her sweater and threw it on the chair. She began rushing around the room opening cabinets, closets, drawers.

"Box?" asked Matt. "What box?"

"A silver lock box," she replied. "If it's here, it may hold the answers I need," said Miranda.

Matt helped Miranda search the entire cottage. They lifted rugs to look for loose floorboards and moved dressers and chests. The thunder clashed and rumbled the walls, the lights flickered. They lighted candles and pressed on with their search.

After a while, however, they were almost ready to give up. Miranda was beginning to feel defeated by her own imagination. She'd believed in such fairytales when she was a girl, but now she was a grown woman, grounded in reality—wasn't she?

She kneeled on the floor of the bedroom. Matt sat on the edge of the bench at the foot of the bed, his hands on his knees.

Suddenly, Miranda recalled a distant memory. It slipped into her conscious mind without warning or effort. The memory was of her grandmother watching her play at the miniature red bridge.

Anna's voice was tender. "You know, I'll bet those fairies really do appreciate you leavin' the food out for them," she'd said.

"Do you really believe in the fairies, Grandma?" asked a young Miranda.

"Of course, I do, child," Anna said. "They're real, and don't you let anyone tell you different."

"I want to believe, but what if it's my imagination?" asked Miranda.

Anna sat down on the grass next to her young granddaughter. "You know what's important in life, Miranda? It's holdin' on to your imagination. 'Cause if you don't let your mind be free, you'll never be able to see what's right in front of your eyes. Do you understand?"

"I think so."

Anna smiled. "Miranda, if you ever start to question what's real, just let go of what you think, and go with what your heart knows to be true."

Miranda snapped out of her dazed recollection; her face was in her hands. Matt came over and gripped her shoulder.

Suddenly, they heard the loudest clash of thunder of the night and the lights went completely out. Miranda stood and walked to the dresser where a candle was lit. She was exasperated. She crossed her arms on the dresser and dropped her head dejectedly. Anna's words rang in her ears once more. '…you'll never be able to see what's right in front of your eyes'.

Miranda opened her eyes and stared down at the white linen runner that covered the dresser. There was a pattern of beautiful primroses stitched upon it. It hit Miranda like a lightning bolt. "Matt!" she cried. Her heart began to race. "The garden! The garden!" She ran from the room and grabbed a small shovel that lay with the garden tools. She hurried past Matt.

"Come to your senses, girl! You can't be goin' out in this storm!" Matt exclaimed.

"I have to!" she replied as she bolted outdoors into the raging downpour.

"Come back, girl! It's not safe! He's coming, I can feel it!" yelled Matt.

Miranda didn't respond to the frightened older man. She had to do this. Matt's pleas became muffled by the pouring rain and by the distance as she hurried across the soaked ground through the darkness. She was headed to the edge of the woods and for her grandmother's favorite primrose garden. It was the oldest one on all of her land.

The wind was fierce, and the rain was unrelenting. The land was dark as pitch, but Miranda knew where she was. She began to dig as fast as she could. Matt was right. She'd fallen in love with Patrick Hyland McShane and she did believe the stories that were told. She was going to follow her heart to find the truth, just like her grandmother taught her. If she could find the box, and if Patrick was right about its contents, then it might prove that everything was true. She was determined to find out.

Miranda's shovel clanked as it hit something metal. She halted abruptly. It had to be the box. She threw the shovel to the side and dropped to the ground. She began to slosh away the mud with her hands until the item was freed from its secret ground.

She could scarcely see for the rain in her face. She tried to wipe her eyes with the back of her soaked hand. The box was indeed locked. The lid felt as if it took a key. Something inside the box slid around as she moved it. She was determined to tear into the thing now. She stood and felt for the shovel and commenced beating the box, hammering until something broke. She sat on her knees, drenched, and winded, her adrenaline high. She couldn't hear her own pants for breath over the downpour.

She placed her hands on the box, the rain washed away much of the mud. The lid was open. She slowly reached inside and felt it–a small chain. There was a pendant attached. Patrick was right. She closed her eyes and clasped it to her heart. She was elated, but suddenly the emotion was clouded with terror. If this was real, then everything was real. Fear consumed her. The incident; the dullahan; Patrick was in danger. She had to find him.

Miranda put the necklace around her neck as she had promised, and quickly made it to her feet. She ran, not toward the cottage, but to the lighthouse. If she could find him anywhere, she hoped it might be there.

She ran across the acreage and to the muddy road. The rain let up slightly but was still fervent. She ran quickly, his name was on her breath. Her heart pummeled her as she sprinted with all her might against the wind and rain. The moon crept from behind the dark clouds and illuminated the road below.

As Miranda ran, she gripped the medallion tightly. "Patrick!" she cried as she neared the lighthouse at top speed, nearly stumbling on the now rocky terrain. "Patrick, where are you?" she screamed.

Suddenly, the ground began to rumble as if it were being pounded with terrific force. There was a sort of hum on the air, an ominous vibration that halted her in her tracks. The storm began to fade away and the earth became eerily silent. Miranda stood in the middle of the road and looked up as something neared. Her lips were parted, her body was frozen. It seemed the horse and rider moved in slow motion as they neared her. All that could be heard was the heaving breaths of the enormous black steed and the thumps of its thunderous gallop. Its breath seethed from its nostrils; its eyes burned red as fire.

Miranda's eyes were stretched to the limit, but she could not move as the great horse approached. As it reached her, the rider yanked the reigns stopping the beast cold. It reared high above her. Its deafening neigh pierced right through to Miranda's core. As the horse's front hooves came crashing down, the rider's appearance became clearer. His cape flowed long and black. His body seemed large and strong. His head was not to be seen.

He leaned forward and began to reach for Miranda. But she lost her grip on the medallion and the moonlight hit it. The rider stopped his motion and pulled back his hand. Miranda caught her breath and tried to run.

She backed away and stumbled, her eyes were fixed upon the sight before her. She struggled to move. But at last, she found her strength and turned away. She ran across the road and through the trees to escape. The rider never moved. Miranda kept looking back, but he remained dauntingly still and seemed to watch her. She dashed through the darkness, scrambling through the thick shrubbery, not wanting to be seen—and suddenly she was grabbed by two incredibly strong and masterful arms. "Patrick!" she screamed.

Miranda was held by the man she loved. She could feel him breathing as she embraced him, her cheek against his chest. Her heart was still pounding fast. For what was merely an instant, she forgot about the horrific encounter on the road. She felt safe in Patrick's arms. But her fear soon returned, and she began to panic once more. She looked up at Patrick's face and he was staring past her, hard into the distance. Miranda turned while still in his arms and saw the horseman between the trees. He was still on the road, his body faced them. But suddenly, he reared his horse into the air once more and shot off like a light down the dark, muddy road.

Miranda was speechless and still shaken, and Patrick at first remained unmoved. Miranda noticed the air seemed to get lighter; the ominous presence seemed to have gone. It was then that Patrick released her, and he looked down at her in the darkness. He could scarcely see her bewildered face. His voice was firm, but indignant. "Why did you come here, Miss Kelly? Why?"

She grabbed hold of him firmly and tried to see his eyes. "Because I love you," she lamented. "I love you, Patrick."

He seemed staggered. "No…" he breathed. "Don't say that. You've got to go back to where you came from." He backed up slightly and turned away. "It isn't safe for you here."

She reached for him. "Patrick, I won't leave!" She grabbed tightly to her necklace. "Look—I found the medallion, just like you told me to…"

Her voice began to trail off and he turned his head slightly toward her as he listened.

"Patrick, I know how old you're supposed to be… and I know what happened to you."

Patrick turned to face her, but he did not speak.

She continued with her desperate plea. "I want to know how you were able to live. I want to know what you are, and what he wants with you. I am not afraid. And even if you don't have the same feelings for me, I will not leave your side."

Patrick's heart was heavy. "You don't know what you're saying," he warned. "You must get as far away from me as you can. I should never have—"

Miranda's heart ached suddenly. "You should never have what?" she asked hesitantly. But she didn't really want his answer. She took one step back and absentmindedly held on to the medallion.

He could see that she was hurt by his words and had misunderstood them. He took her by the shoulders and pulled her nearer to him. "Miranda, that's not what I meant."

Suddenly, he dropped to his knees; his voice was full of emotion. "My only regret is that I put you in danger. And I do have the same feelings for you... because you took my breath away the moment we met; because my heart aches for you when we aren't together; and because your smile fills my soul with such a light that I cannot see anything else. I feel too much for you, Miranda. That's why you have to leave. I would spare you the tortured existence I am about to lead."

Miranda nearly fell into his arms, but the couple was interrupted by loud voices. It sounded like a group of men calling out her name. Two of the loudest voices were familiar. They were Matt and O'Malley.

"Go, Miranda, go!" Patrick said as he stood and tried to force her away.

She grabbed onto him and pulled his face near. This time their kiss was more passionate, more fervent than ever before. This kiss was one of unremitting true love. His hands ran across her soaking mane, hers held tightly to his neck, and then, slowly and reluctantly, they parted. As the group of men drew nearer, Patrick slipped quickly away and disappeared into the darkness.

Chapter Thirteen

觉觉

Pitchforks

Miranda wanted to go after Patrick, but her instincts sent her to quickly meet with the older men at the road. She was still quite flummoxed by her experience but for a moment found humor in what she saw before her. It was Matt, O'Malley, and four other men about their age. They carried various weapons, from muskets to big sticks.

She was stopped in her tracks. "What century is this?" she asked.

"What do you mean?" asked O'Malley.

"I mean, all you're missing are the pitchforks and torches," she replied sardonically while carefully looking around to make sure the dullahan had gone.

Matt came forward. "This is no time for jokin', Miranda. If you'd seen what we've seen tonight… well, well, just where in blazes have you been? We've been searching the whole darned country for you!"

Miranda wasn't sure how much she could–or should say. She didn't want to mention Patrick, but thoughts of the formidable horseman returned and hit her suddenly. "I saw him," she explained.

"Saw who, Miranda?" O'Malley asked anxiously. He stepped forward quickly and took her by the shoulder.

All the men's eyes were wide with trepidation.

"The horseman!" she blurted.

"No!" Matt exclaimed.

The men began to murmur, and then they circled around her and turned to look about. Their weapons were at the ready.

"You saw him?" Matt asked, anxiously looking over. "What did he do? Did he see you? Are you all right?"

"Yes! I'm fine–" she began.

"We've got to get out of here!" one man exclaimed.

"I agree with Liam," said another. "He could come back!"

Matt stared intently into Miranda's eyes. "What were you even doing out here? You left in the rain and you didn't come back, then we saw the dreadful dullahan ourselves and—"

"I was just out for a walk," she said calmly, hoping not to raise suspicion.

Matt and O'Malley looked at each other and back to Miranda. Matt's brow was raised, but he didn't question her aloud. He did, however, share with her an intense look of knowing. He remembered clearly the conversation they had earlier and hadn't forgotten her feelings for Patrick. He knew very well where she'd gone in the storm, and it wasn't for a stroll down the lane. Then he noticed the gold medallion around her neck and marched to her side. "Come with us, Miranda. We've got to get off this road and somewhere safe, where we can have a talk!" Matt insisted.

O'Malley looked at her perceptively and she wondered how much Matt had already told him. She followed the men back to her cottage where their trucks were parked. Matt and O'Malley stayed with Miranda, while Liam and the others took leave to their homes where they would lock up and await further notice.

Once they were inside, Miranda went to her room to change into some clean dry clothes and the men waited nervously by the front door. When she returned to them, O'Malley could hold his tongue no longer. He was nearly in tears. "It's really him isn't it? It's our Patrick... you've got to tell me where he is!"

Miranda's eyes shot to him and then to Matt as if to ask how much he'd already said.

"I told him, Miranda," said Matt. "I had to tell him, we loved Patrick! He was one of our own! But it'll stay between us!" he vowed.

Miranda was overwhelmed. She turned away and gripped her arms tight. "I don't know where he is," she spoke softly. So much had happened, and she only just surmised that Patrick was out there all alone. He should be here, with those who love him, she thought to herself. And where he might be safe from the–

"Miranda the hour is upon us!" Matt reminded. "You now know this full well. But there is much more that you don't know. Sweet Anna was wrapped up in this somehow."

Miranda's ears perked up just then. She turned her head to meet his eyes.

"I don't know much else," said Matt. "There's somebody else who could explain it to you better," he concluded.

O'Malley turned to his friend with surprise in his eyes. "You don't mean…?"

"Yes," said Matt. "She's an eccentric old woman, but she's wiser than folks think." He returned his gaze to the troubled young woman. "She was a friend to your grandma, and I think she can help."

O'Malley seemed shaken. He barely uttered the words, "I don't think that's a good—" When Miranda cut him off.

"When do we leave?" she asked.

Matt took his keys from his pocket and led them out the door.

Chapter Fourteen

൭൹

Flora Farrelly

O'Malley was nervous and began to fidget as the three rode in the front of Matt's truck. "Matthew, can't we figure another way? There's got to be somebody else who can tell her things," he pleaded.

Matt's eyes stayed forward on the road. "There's no one else," he insisted. "It's got to be her."

"Well, I don't like this," said O'Malley. "I don't like it one bit. Can't you drop me off before we get too close?" he pleaded.

"Well, I can… if you're not too worried about the horseman," Matt reminded.

O'Malley's eyes grew large. "Oh!" he huffed fretfully. "Never mind, never mind, keep goin', keep goin'!"

Miranda sat between the men and only half-listened to them chatting. She was more concerned with the road ahead, behind, and beside them. She was watching for the horseman. But alas, all she could see was a misty darkness, and the foggy road in front of their headlights.

Matt drove the road through town. Not a person was in sight. Porch lights and lanterns were out, even at the pubs. The land seemed still, uninhabited. He drove them quite a distance into an even darker, wooded, mysterious place. The road narrowed and they veered off onto a path that didn't seem quite wide enough for a car. Little branches clinked against the sides of the old truck. Miranda noticed O'Malley's hand gripping the arm of the door more tightly. His eyes were fixed on his surroundings, and he seemed to resist shouting out.

Soon they came to a stop. The fog was clearing up ahead and Miranda could make out the lighted windows of a small cabin. Matt stepped out of the vehicle and had Miranda follow.

"Where are you going?" O'Malley blurted.

"I'm not going anywhere, so quit your worryin'," said Matt. He then turned to Miranda and took a slow cleansing breath. "She don't like visitors now, so we're gonna wait here. You go on up and explain who you are. She'll talk to you. She and your grandma were real close. We'll wait as long as it takes."

O'Malley's head snapped toward Matt anxiously, but Matt's stern look prevented him from protesting.

"All right," said Miranda. "If you're sure it's okay."

"I'm sure," said Matt. He smiled softly and turned her toward the cabin. "We'll be right here."

He got back into the truck and the two men watched as Miranda made her way to the dark door and began to knock.

She knocked lightly at the door, but no one answered. She knocked a bit louder the next time and the door unlatched and became ajar. She thought someone had opened it, but no one seemed to be there. She gently pushed it further open and called out. There was no response. A large fireplace was burning in the small room, and the heat from it could be felt where she stood. A large pot was hanging above the flame. She stared at it with wonder when suddenly a voice startled her from her thoughts. "Lookin' for somethin', dear?"

Miranda turned around quickly. An elderly woman carrying a basket stood directly behind her. She'd come straight out of the darkness. Her hair was thick and strikingly silver. It hung over her shoulder in a braid down to her knees. But even more startling were her eyes. They were white as snow and looked not directly at Miranda, but seemingly past her. Miranda surmised the woman was blind. She wore a dark gray shawl and dress.

Miranda tried to calm her racing pulse. "Hello. I think I'm here to see you…" she muttered.

"You think?" the woman chuckled humorlessly. "Don't you know? It's dangerous to be out in such a place this time of night without knowing who you came to see. You might find someone you wish you hadn't." Her voice was bold and firm; it was also smooth and sounded younger than she appeared to be. She walked past Miranda and into the cabin. She dropped her basket onto the heavy-looking wooden table in the middle of the room and began to unpack it. "Do you know if you're coming in?" she asked.

Miranda wasn't sure. "May I?" she replied.

"Well, I suppose if you came with Matthew Sullivan, you must be harmless," the woman decided.

Miranda looked back to the truck that was sitting a little way down the drive and wondered how she knew.

"I don't normally take to visitors, especially during the night," said the woman. "But you can come in… explain what you're doin' here," she mumbled. Her eyes never turned to Miranda; she simply went about her business. She took some of the herbs she'd removed from her basket and rinsed them in a basin of water. Next was a potato. She rinsed and began to cut it without peeling. "Saw you looking at my cauldron. Never seen one before?" the lady asked as she cut and dropped pieces of the crop into the large pot.

"Oh," Miranda began as she broke her stare. She remembered staring at the fireplace when the woman had walked up. "Well, not in person. No."

"Good for cooking a lot at once," she explained. "You gonna introduce yourself, little lady?"

"Oh my, yes. Please excuse my rudeness. My name is Miranda… Miranda Kelly."

The old woman stopped chopping and stared at the table before her blankly. Her eyes then shifted more toward Miranda and she put the knife down. "Kelly, you say?" She picked up more of what she'd cut and took it to the pot. She stirred it in silence and then wiped her hands lightly on her skirt. "Do I know you, Miss Kelly?" she said smartly.

"No," Miranda replied. "But I've been told you knew my grandmother. Her name was Anna."

The woman turned sharply to Miranda, and for the first time looked hard into her eyes. She could see her just fine. "Why did you come here?" she demanded in a derisive tone.

"I was told you could tell me some things about my grandmother," she explained.

"You've been told a lot of things." Her eyes narrowed. She looked past Miranda and out the door to Matt's truck. "But you've been told wrong on this one. You'd better leave now. I've got things to do."

"No, please—I need your help," she pleaded. "Just a few questions… please?"

The woman huffed and slowly walked over and slumped down in a large chair. "Shut the door," she ordered.

Miranda shut it quickly and sat in the chair across from the elderly lady. The rich aroma from the cauldron began to permeate the room.

"Before we begin, my name is Flora Farrelly."

Miranda was warmed when she heard her name. Something about her demeanor became softer when she'd said it, and Miranda was comforted by it. "It's truly a pleasure to meet you," said Miranda.

Flora stared at Miranda's face. "You look like her… your grandma… same credulous eyes." She then turned away as if deep in thought. "You really shouldn't be out here this late. It's dangerous," warned Flora. "Let's make this quick, shall we?"

"I've already seen him," said Miranda.

"Seen who?" asked Flora.

"The headless horseman," Miranda replied.

Flora stood quickly. "Then you know about him?" she said with unease.

"Yes."

Flora turned and walked to the window. "Curious... You seem more troubled than afraid," Flora realized. "You have more questions than those about your grandmother, don't you?" she said knowingly.

"Only if you can answer them," Miranda replied.

"Well, I'm afraid I cannot," Flora replied. "All I know is that your mother passed when you were very young, and I am sorry about that. I also know that you spent your summers here with Anna, but your father raised you in America. And so, I can only advise you to return to him straight away."

Miranda stood and neared the lady whose back remained turned to her. "He is dead now too," she said.

Flora turned to meet her. "For that I am truly sorry. But the best advice I can give you is to go home where it is safe."

"I am home," Miranda insisted.

Flora was suddenly struck with suspicion. "There is more to this, isn't there?" she probed. "What keeps you here?"

Suddenly, Miranda recognized the aroma. "Nothing," she lied. "Nothing more than familiarity."

"That is not true…" Flora corrected. She then neared the younger woman in a stalking manner and stared deep into her eyes. She didn't stop until they were nose to nose. Flora's eyes became slits as she searched for answers, and then something caught her eye. It was the gold chain around Miranda's neck. Her eyes became fixed upon it. She could not see the medallion but knew it was there. "You wear the medallion," she blurted.

Miranda stepped back and clasped her hand over the necklace through her shirt. "You know about this?" she asked anxiously.

Flora became nervous. "You must leave! Go back to where you came from!" she urged authoritatively. "I have no more to tell you. And I don't like guests!" She went to the cauldron and began to stir the contents rapidly. "Be gone with you!"

Miranda went quickly to the door as ordered and observed a small broom hanging lengthwise above it. She was about to leave but came to an abrupt halt. She remembered exactly when she'd smelled that aroma before. It was the first night she'd met Patrick. When he'd startled her as he came down the roadway, he carried a basket that smelled delicious. Miranda turned back to the woman immediately. "You know Patrick, don't you?"

Flora dropped her ladle into the pot and turned around. "I don't know who you are talking about," she warned. "Now, you'd better leave like I told you."

"No! You do know him," said Miranda. "Please… You've got to help me!"

Flora walked fast to the other side of the cabin. "I don't have to do anything. You'll leave if you know what's good for you. Get as far away from here as you can!" Her voice was firm and unyielding.

Miranda finally broke down. All the emotions she had tried to fight for days culminated in that moment. "But I love him," she cried as she fell wearily to her knees.

"No…" Flora breathed. Her heart was breaking for both Patrick and Miranda. This was the worst possible news.

Chapter Fifteen

ণ৪৯০

Three Days

Flora turned away from Miranda and held a deep breath for several seconds. She couldn't believe what she'd heard.

Suddenly, Matt and O'Malley barreled into the cabin. They'd seen Miranda fall to her knees and came running from the truck as fast as their legs would take them.

"What have you done to her?" yelled O'Malley, finding courage only in Miranda's defense.

Flora was unmoved. She was very concerned by Miranda's revelation.

Matt grabbed hold of Miranda to see if she was quite well.

"I'm all right," Miranda sobbed.

O'Malley shook nervously, and stayed near the door, but he still couldn't hold his stuttering tongue. "Why… why… she's an old witch!"

Flora turned around then and sighed. "Flattery will get you nowhere with me, Francis O'Malley."

O'Malley tightened his lips and swallowed noticeably. Matt, who knelt by Miranda, glared up at him disparagingly.

Miranda stood slowly. "She didn't hurt me, O'Malley," she declared. She then went over to Flora. She looked into her eyes as a woman, as a woman with a pleading heart.

Flora returned the gaze. Hers was one of tremendous concern. "You truly love him?" she asked. Her brows were raised, her chin high, her cautious white eyes were fixed on the younger woman.

Miranda was acutely aware of the anxiety in her own stomach, the painful aching of worry in her heart, and the longing she felt for Patrick. "I love him," she admitted. "And I will do anything to help him."

Flora slowly released the breath she'd been holding, never parting her lips. She seemed fretted, setback, sorrowful for something. She turned to the burning fireplace. "Then I suppose I'd better explain some things to you. You're in far too deep to turn back now. The three of you… have a seat. And shut my door, Francis."

O'Malley quickly did as told, his eyes never leaving the older woman. The three then sat in chairs around a small table as Flora spread the logs out under the cauldron to lessen the flame. She then joined them. Her face was cool but concerned.

Thunder began to rumble lowly, alerting the four that the storm had not yet completely gone. But it was quiet, and the wind was exceedingly calm. The only other sound was that of the gentle crackling of the fire and Flora's now mellifluous voice.

She stared intently at O'Malley as she spoke, ever aware of his unease. His eyes remained at his lap. "You three have some things in common," she began. "You all know well of the horseman; you care deeply for Patrick Hyland McShane, and you would risk your necks to help him." She then looked to the others. "And risk your necks you shall," she proclaimed.

They understood fully what she meant. O'Malley resisted the urge to grasp his throat at the thought.

"Listen to me, and listen closely," she continued. "Legends of the feared dullahan known as the headless horseman are many. But some are far less known than others. Yes, he seems to appear from nowhere, and yes, he severs the heads of his victims. But the horseman is not an otherworldly creature... he used to be a man. He was an ordinary man who unwillingly gave his life to become the horseman, and so he seeks vengeance."

The three guests gasped. All were quite dazed by those words. The rain began to sheet down upon the cabin.

"What do you mean?" Matt asked abruptly.

"Remain quiet and listen," Flora insisted. "The horseman will repeatedly return, hunting for victims, some say indefinitely. But it is also said that he is constantly looking for someone to take his place. Somehow the horseman knows when he has found the right man. And he will return for him when the time is right."

Miranda's mind was awhirl. Her eyes shifted wildly as she took this in and recognized the connotations in relation to Patrick.

Matt and O'Malley noticed this as well. They recalled the horseman's words clearly. 'I'll be back for you' he'd told their friend.

Miranda listened hard to every word that Flora breathed. She wondered what it was exactly that he wanted with Patrick. Part of her felt weak and sickened by the thoughts that plagued her, but in another way, she felt zealous, wanting to fight for Patrick. She wanted to stop the horseman at any cost. For the moment, physical weakness prevailed. She could hardly lift her eyes as Flora spoke, as tears began to burn them.

Flora stood and removed her shawl. She laid it carefully on the arm of the cushioned chair and took a breath before turning completely away from Miranda. To continue would cause more pain, but she knew she must. She paced the floor slowly.

"The horseman seems to return when the mood strikes him," said Flora, "generally every twenty to thirty years. One can only speculate as to where he goes in between time, maybe other villages, other realms, but he always finds his way back to us, and no one knows his rhyme or purpose. But this time is different. He is later than ever before, and there's a reason for this."

Flora returned her gaze to Miranda's. "Somehow, Anna discovered that the horseman can only be replaced when the new moon aligns in front of the sun forming a ring of fire high above the Emerald Isle. It last happened in nineteen-forty-four, and it will happen again in–"

Miranda abruptly finished Flora's sentence, "three days." She was stagnant for several seconds; her heart had stopped. Then she abruptly pushed herself up from the table as did the flabbergasted men.

Matt had a humbling realization. "What a minute, now. You haven't explained Patrick! How is he still here? Why didn't he die?" he asked shrewdly.

"The headless horseman takes the heads of his victims," Flora reminded. "But he doesn't take the head of the man who will be his successor… until the night he comes back for him."

O'Malley felt faint. He'd always wanted explanations. He'd been chasing after Patrick's ghost for years, knowing he'd seen it. But he usually drank before doing such things. He hadn't drunk a thing this night, and this news was just too much to bear.

"Patrick was chosen," said Flora. Her tone became dark. "For whatever reason, he was chosen. And as such, he is doomed to walk the land, half living and half dead, until the time he takes over as horseman. In the dark of night, he lives as a man. He can eat, he can touch... feel like a man. Under the light of the sun he is merely a presence, unseen and unheard. It is a tortured existence. But when the sun and moon align, forming the ring of fire, his two forms will also be joined, and he will become the one you fear. He will not know you. He will become the headless horseman."

O'Malley gripped the table and held himself up. His head and stomach were shaken and stirred.

Staggered, Matt grasped his heart.

Miranda walked slowly to the fireplace and stared blankly into it. She couldn't see or feel anything but fear and heartache.

Flora interjected one last piece of vital information. "What I've said tonight must stay between the five of us," she insisted.

"The five of us?" asked Matt. "But we're only four," he said.

Flora gazed at Miranda and the young woman suddenly realized what she'd meant. She turned just as thunder clashed and lightning lit the outdoors—and there, standing in the doorway, soaking wet and discontented, was Patrick Hyland McShane. He stared frigidly at his lover and old friends.

O'Malley laid eyes on him and all at once collapsed heavily to the floor.

Chapter Sixteen

❧

Out of the Storm

Flora tended to O'Malley and helped him to a sitting position on the floor. He leaned wearily against the wall. His fear of her was lost. He was much calmer now, but his eyes were wide as he stared on at the site before him. For the first time, Patrick stared back at him, and for the first time there were witnesses to share this hallucination.

Matt wanted to help, but just now his thoughts and most other senses failed him. His eyes were fixed upon a dear friend of old, a man like a brother to him; one whose life had been whisked away so many years ago. He could not speak. He could not think. He could not believe it was Patrick.

Miranda, whose heart was wrenched with pain, felt great peace when she saw the man she loved. She ran to him, and he took her into his arms. She held onto him and tried not to weep. His clothes were wet and cold. She reached for his face and stroked his cool, damp skin. "Patrick, you're here," she uttered tenderly.

"And so are you," he observed. His eyes spoke lovingly, but his tone was firm. "I told you to leave this place," he reminded. He searched her eyes fervidly for any glimmer of reason.

Flora watched as the couple held each other and she knew once and for all it was true love they shared.

At last, Matt found his words. "By the spirits—it's really you." He clutched his heart as he stared on, and Patrick slowly left Miranda's grasp and went to his old friend.

Matt almost stepped back instinctively, but he managed to stay strong and still. Patrick came close and stopped. The two men remained frozen at length and then Patrick suddenly began to smile. His familiar grin washed away all of Matt's fears and quelled those of O'Malley who watched from nearby.

Matt began to weep silently, and Patrick took him by the shoulder. "Don't fret, my good friend," he said consolingly.

Matt looked up into the caring eyes of his old friend, still young in appearance as if no time had passed, and whose words were just like they had always been… kindly and sound. "You're tellin' me not to fret?" Matt began to chuckle. "All you've been through and with the horseman after ya', and you're tellin' me, it'll be all right? By George, it is our Patrick!"

O'Malley wiped his own tears and ambled to his feet. The two older men then embraced Patrick so strongly that it took him by surprise, and he nearly lost his footing.

Soon Flora had them all seated, and Patrick had changed into dry clothes that she had for him in a back room. The stew in the cauldron had been for Patrick to take, yet there was enough for the lot of them. The older men shared a bit while Patrick and Miranda stood by the window and looked out at the rain.

Flora decided it was time to tell the whole truth. She could see that Miranda had no plans to leave Patrick and return to America. It didn't matter what she'd heard so far. Flora would have to tell her the most painful part of this tale: that there was no possible chance for a happy ending. Flora and Patrick both knew this full well.

"Miranda, dear," said Flora as she took a seat. "Come sit with me."

Miranda held tightly to Patrick's hand, memorizing the feel of it. When Flora called her, she gripped his hand tighter, then, gingerly released her grasp. She sat across from the old woman, and unknowingly, her hand still clenched as if to hold onto Patrick's touch.

Flora took notice of this. Then her eyes washed over the young lady. She spoke so that everyone would hear, but so that Miranda would truly listen. "Miranda, you have true love in your heart, and love in its purest form will always overcome wisdom."

Miranda was paused by those words. She'd heard this tone before, and not once, but twice. She felt she knew where Flora was heading, but for the moment said nothing.

Flora continued. "I know you will not listen to reason, so you will have to hear the painful truth. There is no life for you here, no happiness...

only pain and anguish. I wish it were not true, but it is. Patrick cannot fight the horseman. In three days, he will take his place."

The storm rumbled lowly outside, and the rain drops slowly began to fade in their part of the forest.

"How can you say this?" Miranda asked sorrowfully. "He can fight—or he can hide!"

"That's right!" Matt exclaimed. "We can do something! We can't just let it happen!"

"Your hearts are true, and your intentions are noble, but you don't understand," Flora insisted. "Patrick cannot run from the horseman. It isn't possible. He will find him. And he cannot fight him and win. What will be, will be."

Matt stood and pounded his fist on the table. "I won't hear that!" he blasted. "What if he leaves with Miranda to the States 'til the confounded eclipse is gone?"

"That's right!" said O'Malley, standing alongside his friend.

"I cannot leave this place," Patrick said painfully. "I am cursed to roam these lands until my time has come." He looked hard into the eyes of Miranda telling her it was true.

A hush fell over the room. Miranda stood. She was utterly stunned. She didn't know what to say, or to ask. Patrick came to meet her and took her carefully by the shoulders. He roamed her eyes with his piercing emerald gaze. His face revealed a sadness Miranda had not noticed before. It was one of long-felt desolation.

"I must find a way," Miranda whispered charily. Her heart ached as she thought of Patrick's despair. "I won't let it happen."

Flora had stood from her chair and was lighting some candles and black sage. "Miranda, have you heard the legends of the banshee women?" she asked.

"Flora!" Patrick boomed. His look was as hard and cold as stone. "No," he beseeched.

"I must, Patrick. She is in too deep already," said Flora.

"Yes!" he exclaimed. "She is in too deep, and it ends here," Patrick warned.

Everyone froze still as Patrick's booming voice quaked the cabin. Not even Flora said a word.

Patrick returned his gaze to Miranda. This time he kneeled and pleaded. "Miss Kelly, you must leave here. After all you've heard, all you now know—don't wait a minute longer. I beg of you." His voice was deep and powerful, but full of hurt. And he couldn't look into her eyes when he said the last words, "Go... and never come back."

She stroked his hair tenderly as his head hung low. "All right, Patrick," she finally breathed. "I'll go."

His eyes quickly shot back to hers, but he stared cautiously.

"I'll go," she repeated. "If you let Flora tell me everything she knows, and my feelings change."

He closed his eyes and drew a weak and agonizing breath. He then stood to his full towering height. His jaw was tight. His lips did not part. He backed away from her, looked over to his friends, and then left the cabin without a word.

Tears burned Miranda's eyes. She turned to follow him, but Flora grabbed her by the arm.

"Let him go, lass," Matt said tenderly. "Stay here and listen to what Flora has to say. Time is runnin' out."

Chapter Seventeen

∞

Banshees

Miranda felt a part of her slip away, every time he walked out the door. She knew now more than ever that she would be bound to him always, somehow, some way.

She'd returned to this land, not sure if she'd ever want to leave again. She'd been drawn to revisit Kilcrohane, and with hopes she would find herself again... but she found considerably more. She'd found love; a love she was sure had been waiting for her, unbeknownst to either of them. Yet, here they were, trapped in a harrowing, formidable fantasy.

She'd questioned her heart, and even her sanity. But that was over. In a short time, she'd discovered truth in the implausible: the existence of the murderous dullahan, a sorrowful tale of a friendship and life lost, and even more, she found unparalleled true love.

And she now knew the entire truth about Patrick. She knew why she'd only seen him at night. She knew what he was trying to protect her from. He didn't turn out to be the man she first thought he was… no, he was infinitely more than she ever would have dared to dream. He was everything to her. And no matter what laid ahead for him, she was determined to stand by his side and bear it with him.

She turned abruptly to Flora; her tears now gone. "Tell me everything," she said firmly.

Flora's lips curved into a soft but reluctant grin. "Yes, everything," she replied. "Come now. Have a seat." She then carefully poured each of them a cup of tea.

Matt and O'Malley returned to their chairs next to Miranda at the table. Flora strolled along the floor as she spoke, her hands folded, her mind forming every thought. She wanted to explain it as clearly as she could.

Miranda and the gentlemen relaxed unwittingly as they took in the gentle perfume of the burning sage smudge stick. They listened carefully to Flora's words.

"I asked you before if you remember any tales of the banshees. Do you?" she asked.

"Yes," said Miranda. "I heard stories when I was a girl."

"What do you know about them?" asked Flora.

"Only that they are wailing women, maybe even fairy women, who alert of a coming death," Miranda explained.

Flora stopped pacing and turned to the table. "All legends sprout from the seed of truth. But much can easily be lost in translation. And, I suppose, in interpretation." Her look seemed harder than before. Her brow was furrowed. "Have you heard of their relation to the dullahan—the headless horseman?"

The others looked at each other with question in their eyes.

"No," said Miranda.

"Do you have anything stronger to drink?" O'Malley interjected frankly. "Maybe just a little drop of somethin' for my tea," he asked. His anxiety was returning very quickly.

Flora kept talking while she slipped a tiny silver bottle from the pocket of her dress and poured a bit of something into his cup. He stared into it and then to Matt. He was unsure but drank it anyway.

Flora continued. "There are many tales, but one says the banshees wail when the horseman has named his next victim. That's how you know there will be a death. But that is not exactly the case… at least not always. Not many know what I am about to tell you, girl. And this is what Patrick doesn't want you to know." She paused for a moment before continuing. "You see, Miranda, often, the wailing banshee is a grieving woman. She's not wailing because the horseman's found a victim. The screams folks hear are the cries of the horseman's lover, parted from him forever. Upon his return, she screams his name and pleads for his memory. But he knows naught. No matter how she tries, he will never know her; he will only know retribution and death. The wailing of the banshee is the horrified yell of a weeping, tortured, soul. And when she dies her spirit will go into the hills, where she will weep for him still."

Miranda's legs were weak as she tried to stand and get away. The two men tried to brace her, but she stumbled away from them.

Flora knew it was a painful revelation to Miranda, but she also knew there was no other way to make her comprehend what would happen if she stayed.

Miranda was dazed. Even up to now she saw light at the end of the tunnel, but it was fading quickly, and she couldn't let it. This was too much. This meant there truly was no hope, only despair. She would not, could not accept it. She didn't have to share the same fate as others. It would be different for her, she anxiously told herself.

Flora stepped closer to the young woman. "Miranda... Anna loved the horseman," she said.

"What?" said Miranda. She breathed hard and backed against the wall. She was confused, but she could not absorb another painful thought. She couldn't consider Flora's allegation or how it was possible. "No," she mouthed, as she tried to make it to the door.

"It is true!" Flora insisted. "And she tried everything in her power to make him remember! Just like all the women before her! But it was not to be!"

Miranda tumbled out the door in effort to escape. Matt and O'Malley ran swiftly after her and Flora came to the door.

"I wish it weren't true, Miranda – but she spent a lifetime loving him and it killed her! You must leave as Patrick would spare you this pain!"

Miranda ran into the woods at full speed. Matt and O'Malley were no match. They had no choice but to stop.

She ran east, west, anywhere to escape. She could see nothing but blackness. All she could hear were Flora's horrific words blaring loudly in her ears, over and over. She became weak, overwhelmed. She stumbled onto a muddy road and was lost. She then collapsed, and all sounds faded.

Chapter Eighteen

ೞಬಬ

A Touch in the Dark

Miranda's subconscious took hold, and to her, all was dark. She could see nothing, no thoughts pervaded her. The familiar sound of footsteps on lush grass was all she could sense, and the subdued sensation of floating along. But soon, those feelings faded as well.

After a time, her eyes slowly opened. It was dark, and she was in her bed, seemingly alone. Only the faintest sliver of moonlight showed through the windowpane and reached the doorway to the bath.

She slid to her bare feet and stared into the dark at where the floor should be. She ambled mindlessly about the shadowy room trying desperately to push aside her disparaging thoughts for at least a few moments. As she wearily tried to fend them off, she stripped her clothing and made way to the claw-foot bathtub. She turned on a hot shower and stumbled into it, never lighting the small room.

The searing water soothed her but could not keep away her tears. Her legs became weak as she knelt under the water and began to weep. Every memory since she'd returned to Ireland now pained her. The memories of Patrick hurt the most, for he had touched her deepest. She indeed loved him, and the realization of what he was, and what he was to become, finally rocked her to the core—and all at once.

Her head hung low as she cried, her hand held tightly to the curved edge of the cast-iron tub. She thought nothing could ease her pain. But then, he touched her hand.

Her heartache had so overwhelmed her that his sudden presence in the moonlit room did not frighten her. On the contrary, nothing could have soothed her more.

Her tears stopped but she could not speak. His hand caressed hers as he knelt before her and no words were shared between them. Everything she had learned that night had suddenly become a part of her; the thoughts melded together, not as a string of events, but as a deplorable feeling, a burden that belonged to Patrick—and one she had decided to share.

He knew that she would not leave him. And he'd known it would be even truer if she ever heard about the unending determinations of the wailing women. As much as it pained him, he knew that her love for him would cause her to stay. And there was nothing to be done about it now.

Both Patrick and Miranda stood. The steam surrounded them. Somehow in the near-dark they could see into each other's eyes, into each other's souls. They shared a passionate kiss; one that would speak for them the words they could not manage. Her lips were warm and wet; his mouth took hers eagerly and sweetly. Tears streamed down her face, she'd never wanted him or needed him more than now. She forced his clothing from him as they kissed, and he joined her under the hot water.

His lips left hers only to relish the softness of her neck and the wet of her hair. As he tenderly pressed her against the wall, the water pouring over them gracefully, she held onto him for dear life, and would never let go. He soon lifted her thirsting body to meet him, and, for a time they hoped would last forever, they escaped to a world of passion and tranquility where no one and nothing could keep them apart.

Chapter Nineteen

ෆ෪ඎ

Dust to Dust

The couple lay amongst the white linens of her bed, nude and lovingly entwined; their souls momentarily at peace while they slept in each other's shielding embrace. Miranda emerged slowly from her slumber and her eyes surveyed Patrick's face. His look was stern as he slept. She memorized every detail adoringly, from the reds of his brows to the curve of his lips.

He opened his eyes and gazed into hers. She drank him in wholly and allowed his essence to fill her being. But suddenly, something else caught her attention. The sun was beginning to rise.

She'd never seen Patrick during the day; a fact she had not discerned until Flora explained Patrick's particular affliction. The older woman had said, 'in the dark of night he lives as a man... under the light of the sun he is merely a presence, unseen and unheard…'

Miranda held onto him tighter, but as the room became less dim, she felt his muscles tense and his eyes turned away from her. He'd realized he'd overstayed and didn't want her to see him change. She knew this and with all her heart wanted him to stay. She stared at him; her arms wrapped firmly around his neck.

When his eyes met her stare, she pleaded. "Don't go. We are one now. I want to share in every part of your existence. Please let me hold you as long as I can." Her heart was heavy, her hold was unrelenting.

He strengthened his embrace as the light became brighter. "I'll still be here," said Patrick. His voice was weaker than she had ever heard it before. It nearly broke with emotion. "You won't know it, but I'll be here."

Tears stung her eyes. "I'll know it, Patrick. I'll feel you with me…"

They kissed deeply, meaningfully. Soon, his physical body began to fade before her eyes, and it transformed into many orbs of golden light. She was breathless. The balls of light then merged into one pulsing luminous orb. Then it suddenly burst like a dying star into particles of radiant dust that fell upon her and slowly vanished.

She was heartbroken again, and winded. She couldn't blink. She touched her lips in remembrance of his kiss and felt the sheets where he had just laid. She felt as if in a tidal wave. She'd been awakened to many unfathomable truths in recent hours and had been overwhelmed by each. But this time was different. This time something burned within her. It was love and it was hardcore determination.

She went to the window and watched as the rays of the rising sun in the east stretched out to the western sea before her. Her cheeks were streaked with tears, but her eyes began to narrow. Patrick Hyland McShane might have resigned to his fate, but Miranda Kelly was determined to find a way to save him.

Chapter Twenty

☙❧

Old Letters

Miranda spent the morning going through her grandmother's old papers, books, anything she could find that might reveal information about the horseman or what she knew about him. Then she remembered searching with Matthew the night of the storm. She recalled that the bench at the foot of the bed was also a chest. The lights had gone out that night, but beforehand she had come across some old papers and things in the chest. She hadn't paid much attention as her focus was the silver lock box.

She went to the chest and opened it. It smelled fresh of lavender sachets and cedar. In the daylight she could see some old letters and a worn-looking leather-bound book. Anxiously, she took them to the bed and carefully looked them over. The book was in fact a journal. Miranda thumbed through it at first. The last few pages that showed writing were covered from top to bottom, front and back, with the same repeating sentence: *'He knew my name.'*

Miranda was haunted by those words. Those pages were particularly worn, somewhat brittle and partly stained from wetness. She pondered whether the damage had been caused by tears.

She went to the beginning and began to read intently. The first words, "20 May 1944: Death is but a barrier, our love will endure". Had Anna at first accepted the passing of her lover? If she had, the tone of the journal gingerly began to change over time. It became apparent that she had not accepted his death; that she was in a constant battle between her undying love for a man named Seamus Blackstone, and keeping the ultimate secret: that he had become the headless horseman. That clandestine detail would remain such in order to protect his good name; and for the sake of herself and of her child.

As Miranda read on, she discovered that Anna had become pregnant by a man who promised to marry her, but he'd left her instead. She then met Seamus and embarked on what seemed a whirlwind romance. He wanted to marry her and claim the child as his own, but that dream was not to be, for he was cut down under the ring of fire by the merciless dullahan.

Miranda's heart was warmed when Anna described life raising her beloved daughter, and it was torn when she candidly spoke of the pain of wanting the horseman to return so she could have another chance to try and save him. '*If only I could summon him,*' she had written, '*and bestow an adoring embrace that would shatter the hindrances and return him to me.*'

Tears now stung Miranda's eyes. Her grandmother had written of the terror she felt when he had finally come, and how her love for him all but erased those fears even as he delivered his horrible vengeance on the village. He'd slaughtered several, including Patrick.

Miranda closed the journal quickly and took a deep breath. She wanted to learn everything she could, but reading her grandmother's account of Patrick's death would be yet another painful experience.

She tried to collect herself, but the feeling of loss began to pierce her heart. She held the book against her, her eyes closed tight. She fought hard against the hurt she was feeling inside.

Suddenly, a soothing breeze glided across Miranda's arms and wrapped around her like a warm embrace. All at once she felt more at ease. Patrick was with her. And just as she'd promised, she could feel him.

Chapter Twenty-One

ⁿⁿⁿ

The Journal

Miranda finished reading her grandmother's journal, scouring over every fine detail. She opened the letters and read them as well. Some were letters she'd written to her grandmother when she was a girl. She was moved that her grandmother had kept them. A tear fell from her eyes, and as she wiped it, she had a revelation. For all of the letters, even the few from Seamus Blackstone during their brief time together, something was missing–conspicuously so. There were no notes about the horseman in later years, no mention of Patrick after he was chosen, nothing to tell of her researching a way to break the dullahan's curse. She felt there had to be something more, and yet it was not there. The only hint was the chilling statement that was rewritten dozens of times on the final pages, 'He knew my name."

She got up and paced the floor throughout the small house. She hadn't much to go on. Where would she turn to next? How could she find out any more than she already had–any more than her grandmother had? Then something came to mind. Today's technology was something her grandmother was not accustomed to, but Miranda was. However, would it help in a case such as this? Could a person actually search for the headless horseman on the internet and learn how to stop him?

It was truly a long shot, Miranda understood. But she would try anything. She pulled out her laptop, something she'd hoped she wouldn't have to do on this trip. Now, the stresses of her other home seemed trite, and she was no longer concerned with any of the things that used to plague her. She'd begun a new life and was focused on spending it with the one she loved.

She connected the computer to her mobile network and began to peruse the web.

She found quite a bit of information on the horseman, many different legends. A few were even similar to what Flora had explained. But she learned nothing she felt was of use in this case—until she added a name to her search: Patrick Hyland McShane.

The name Hyland was a match to a very interesting tale, albeit a short one. It was on an old family tree webpage that hadn't been filled in, let alone finished. The page was full of broken links and ads, and the author was not named. The page described what seemed to be a familial legend. It was explained as something which had been previously written in old Irish Gaelic and had been translated into a chilling poetic statement. It read:

> Beware of Dorian Hyland.
> He rides at night 'til cold blood runs,
> A lot which will befall his sons.
> Though lifetimes he may lie in wait,
> The ring of fire will seal their fate.

Suddenly, someone knocked three times at the door. Miranda jumped with fright. Her hand calming her chest, she opened the door. It was Flora.

"I brought something for you," she said in a dejected tone. Then, before Miranda could invite her in, she stepped inside and handed her a small blue book. "It was Anna's. It will explain more than I could. She gave it to me not long before she–" Flora couldn't speak of Anna's death just now, not in light of recent events, including Miranda's blind willingness to share her grandmother's fate. "She wanted it safe. It's everything she knew about the horseman, and also about Patrick. I just thought you ought to have it." She then turned to walk away.

"Thank you," said Miranda. "I was hoping for something like this. It might help," she said after the woman.

Flora turned and looked at Miranda sternly in the eyes. "There's naught to help you now, child." Then Flora walked away, leaving Miranda in silence.

The hours ticked away relentlessly. As the afternoon passed, the sky became darker. Thick gray clouds swam across the sky, possibly warning of another storm.

Miranda sat on the step outside the door of the cottage and read the book Flora had given her. She read slowly, critically, and when she was finished, she read it again. The book was another handwritten account of events, but more abridged in its details. It was very much a list of simplified notes. To Miranda, certain remarks stood out from the others.

There were several entries in which she spoke of Patrick. The most profound was how she'd found him wandering, lost and confused the night after his death. 'He knew naught of his death 'til I found him. He is overcome, desolate. Only I can understand his plight. Flora and I will care for him, and forever keep his secret.'

The writing told of the use of herbs and tinctures she'd used to try and cure Patrick's affliction, and of his beginning to accept his fate. But one particular entry stopped Miranda in her tracks the second time she read it. It had been underlined multiple times, but she didn't realize the connotations of the statement until just now. '1 October 1992, Seamus's birthday - someone else has been to his grave.'

"Wait a minute–" Miranda breathed aloud. "'Someone else'? She doesn't mention it again. Did she ever find out who it was?"

Miranda stared blankly into the distance, deep in thought. Suddenly, the breeze began to pick up and the pages on her lap began to rapidly turn. She quickly stopped the papers and stared at the words on the last page. A connection emerged that hadn't before. The words were: 'Seamus is the key.' It was dated a week before Anna's death.

Miranda abruptly stood. The speed of the wind increased, and she held her hair back from her eyes. "Seamus. Someone visited Seamus's grave. She must have seen evidence of this. And Seamus is the key–"

Could it be that simple? Could there be someone else in Kilcrohane who knew Seamus well enough to visit his grave? His letters mentioned nothing of other friends, or even relatives. She would have to look into this straight away.

The thunder began to rumble, and day was passing into dusk. Miranda went inside and raced to her computer. She searched for Blackstones in Kilcrohane. None were listed. She looked for periodicals and other records regarding Seamus's death. She could find no obituaries which might name friends and relatives, no old news clippings, no records online for the small village. She then recalled her first visit from Matt Sullivan when she'd arrived. 'I know all the folks around these parts,' he'd said.

She was going about this all wrong. In a small town, the people are the source. She'd have to get to Matthew right away.

It was getting quite dark. Miranda turned on the double globe lamp on the side table and grabbed her keys. She ran for the door and when she swung it open, someone gently gripped her arm from behind. "Going without saying goodbye?" Patrick said softly.

Miranda turned around and fell into his arms. He'd returned, and she could hold him again. All other thoughts momentarily ceased.

Chapter Twenty-Two

CRSO

Dance with Me

Patrick stood tall, looking down into the loving eyes of Miranda. He pushed the curly locks of hair from her face, his eyes memorizing her every feature, her skin, her lips, her nose, her eyes. He seemed to be drinking her in, to memorize her for all time.

Miranda was intoxicated by his presence. He was pleasingly warm to her touch; his stare was inviting. She remembered how he'd slipped away only hours before, yet it seemed like days. She never wanted to feel that again. And she knew they had no time to lose. If she wanted to be with him forever, she would have to find a way to save him. Her lips slowly parted. "Patrick," she whispered. "I found some things… I… I want to check them out…"

Patrick didn't respond right away; he leaned down and pressed his lips against her forehead. He then kissed her cheek, her hair, her neck, savoring her scent, her taste, the feel of her.

She dropped her keys as his mouth covered hers. He kissed her with such passion that they momentarily drifted away to another realm.

When he broke the kiss, he took her hand. "Come outside," he said softly. "Dance with me."

Miranda was taken aback. She smiled with surprise as he led her out under the night sky. "But Patrick, what about–"

"Miranda," he said with great sincerity. "We're running out of time. Dance with me." He smiled.

Tears threatened Miranda's eyes. She knew the truth in this. She knew that Patrick had accepted what would happen to him and didn't want to waste a single moment. She gripped his hand tighter and followed him to dance under the stars.

He took her into his arms.

"Patrick, there's no music," said Miranda.

"Then I will sing to you," he replied.

As they danced, he began to sing a tender, soulful tune she had never heard. She fell in love with him all over again. Both love and pain pierced her heart. She was beginning to feel that the two sensations were one in the same.

His words took her breath away. She never wanted to leave her place in his loving embrace. Tears slowly streamed from her eyes and the rain began to pour. She stretched out her arms and welcomed the flow of the soothing rain drops on her face. He twirled her around then lifted her into his arms for another affectionate kiss.

Soon they went inside, removed their wet clothing and lay together by the burning fireplace. They simply enjoyed each other, memorized each other, and shared their love the whole night through.

Chapter Twenty-Three

☙❦❧

The Cemetery

Shortly after dawn, Miranda called Matt and asked him where Seamus had been buried. Matt told her where to meet him. It was cold this morning, and foggy, difficult to see the road ahead. The sky seemed low and was eerily gray.

Miranda parked alongside Matt's truck but didn't see him. She climbed out of her car and holding her sweater tightly around her, made her way across the soft green grass.

There was an old stone structure, still partly standing after what must have been several centuries, and the ground was dotted with headstones, some just as old, some new.

Matt appeared beside an elder tree and waved her near. "Over here, Miranda. Is this what you're lookin' for?" he asked.

There, at the end of a row of headstones was a small one, laid flat on the ground and settled beneath a crown of overgrown blades of grass. 'Seamus Blackstone', it read, '1912-1944'.

"Matt, I wanted to look at the headstones surrounding Seamus's to see if there are family members here; and to ask if you're familiar with the name."

"Oh, boy… Blackstone," he mumbled as he searched his memory. "Not in Kilcrohane. Didn't even know much about Seamus. I think he was one of them world-travelers. Wasn't 'round here much… 'til close to the end I suppose."

They shared an unintentional moment of silence.

"Maybe these are his parents' graves," Miranda suggested looking over the previous two headstones.

They were older, and bore the names Brier Blackstone and Muireann Blackstone, wife of Brier.

"Must be related," said Matt. "Seein' as they're together. Seamus was the only Blackstone I remember hearin' about."

Miranda thought hard for a moment. "By the look of these headstones, Muireann and Brier died long ago," she said. "That means someone else must have known Seamus. Grandma wrote in her journal that someone visited his grave in 1992. She must have seen flowers there or something."

"Maybe it was just a friendly passerby, doin' a good deed," said Matt. "Could've been a coincidence."

Miranda sighed. "I'm starting to think there are no coincidences, Matt," she said. "Maybe he had a sibling."

"You'd be right, Miranda," chimed a familiar voice nearby.

They turned to see that Flora had joined them.

"How did you know we were here?" asked Miranda.

Flora looked at her sternly. "I promised Patrick that I would look after you," said Flora. "And I'll do just that—futile as it may be."

Miranda understood her tone but disregarded it just now. "You said I was right about something, what did you mean?" she asked.

Flora seemed to grit her teeth. She looked at Matt and then reluctantly to the young woman and took a deep breath. "Seamus had a sister," she admitted, to Matt and Miranda's great surprise.

"A sister!" Miranda exclaimed.

"Yes," said Flora. "She lives in Durrus."

"Lives?" Miranda wondered aloud. She recalled the birth date on Seamus's headstone, and he was twelve years older than her grandmother. "How old is she?"

"Ninety-seven," answered Flora. "I've only met her once. And she was not very friendly. Anna found out about her and visited her several times near the end. What they spoke of, I do not know. But I am sure of this: whatever she learned from that woman shortened Anna's path to death."

"Take me to her," Miranda insisted.

"Absolutely not," Flora said flatly.

"Then I shall go there myself, and knock on every door until I find her," Miranda said with a turn toward her car.

Matt went after her and Flora remained where she stood. "Why can't you see?" Flora asked despairingly. "There is no way to stop this. You're on the same painful path as your grandmother, one that can only lead to more despair, and ultimately your death." She turned away, her own grief over Anna's demise resurfacing, and unwilling to see it happen to Anna's beloved granddaughter.

Miranda returned to her. "It was meant to be," she said softly.

Flora turned to her, confused by her words.

Miranda simply said what was in her heart; something she'd just come to realize. "It was always meant to be this way. I was meant to come home, to meet him, to fall in love with him. There are no coincidences. And now that I have him, I will not let go. And if I cannot save him, then I despair anyway, I will die anyway. But I have until tomorrow to try and live."

For the first time, Flora and Matt both felt they understood. They understood what Anna had gone through, and what Miranda bore now.

Flora's eyes were wet with tears. She gently lifted her hand to Miranda's face and nodded. "Then let us go to Durrus," she agreed.

Chapter Twenty-Four

☙❧

Imogen

Miranda, Flora, and Matt took his truck back to Miranda's cottage and rode together to Durrus. Though the skies were gray and the colorful rolling landscapes were muted by fog, the region was beautiful, serene. But Miranda's perspective had changed since she first arrived. This time she had an even broader sense of Ireland's allure, its magic. It was more than a magnetic charm. She realized it was enchanting, even supernatural.

They arrived at a little cottage by the bay, which was framed by mossy stones and crowded with shrubbery. Wisps of fog drifted past the doorway and a woman appeared there. One hand was on her hip, the other on a withered-looking wooden cane. She gave a good stare at her guests as they climbed out of the car. "You might as well come in," she mildly huffed. "I've been expecting you." She slowly turned and went back inside.

The woman's face showed her age, but her movements did not. Miranda thought she was rather spry for ninety-seven and she was quite impressed. But she remembered what Flora had said about her personality, and she wondered how it was that she knew they would be coming.

They stepped inside as instructed and followed the elderly woman's voice. She led them to a back room which had a long row of windows that overlooked the fog-covered bay. A fireplace was burning and two ornately decorated table lamps lighted the sitting area of the room. The woman sat next to the fire in an armchair and stared conspicuously at her company. Her hair was thick and braided like Flora's, but only as long as her shoulders. Much of it was white and surprising touches of natural red were still apparent. Her face was kindly, but Miranda wondered if her looks could be deceiving.

"Flora Farrelly, we meet again," she said with disdain in her voice.

Flora responded while taking her seat in a chair. "Imogen," Flora croaked with effort. "A pleasure, I'm sure," she finished, her voice hinting at sarcasm.

Both women realized their distaste for each other, even though they'd met just once. During that first meeting it was made clear that Imogen didn't care much for people and Flora hadn't responded to that very well. From that day forward, Anna had visited Imogen alone, and it always worried Flora. Soon afterward, Anna died. The two women hadn't seen each other since.

Matt and Miranda sat on the sofa. "My name is Miranda Kelly, Mrs...." she began.

"Just Miss Blackstone," said Imogen. "Never had a husband; never wanted one. Never had much use for men," she proclaimed, while staring directly into Matt's eyes.

A shiver went up his spine.

"But enough with the pleasantries," Imogen said with a grin. "Let's get down to business. I know who you are because I heard from someone in your little village that Anna's granddaughter was in town. I knew it had to be you when I saw you with Flora. And I knew, with the horseman being back same time as you, questions would be raised, and somehow you would end up here, just like your Anna. You want to know about her death, right?"

Miranda was in shock. "Her death?" she asked. "Why no, she died of sickness."

Imogen's eyes went quickly to Matt and Flora. "Is that what they told you?" She seemed somewhat bemused herself.

Miranda's back straightened.

"This is enough," spat Flora. "She didn't come here to talk about this. She came to ask you about Seamus."

"He is the horseman, you can say it," Imogen said in a dark tone. "I'm fully aware of what he is, and of what Patrick will become."

Matt was surprised to hear that Imogen knew as much about Patrick, but Flora wasn't as shocked. "How can you be so cavalier—" Flora began. But she was cut short by Miranda.

"Wait!" the young woman exclaimed. "First things first! What's this about my grandmother's death?" She looked at Matt. "No more secrets…"

He couldn't lie when he looked into her eyes. "You're right, Miranda," he agreed.

"Matthew–" Flora interjected.

Matt held up his hand in his defense. "No, it's time she knew. Now this is the only thing I've kept from you, I swear it. Miranda… Anna didn't just die from illness, she… she walked into the sea during a raging storm. Flora was with her. She tried to stop her, but she couldn't. Then, somehow—I don't know how in the world she did it—but she got her out of the water safely. Anna just took ill from the cold." Matt's eyes fell to the floor after recalling the terrible memory.

Flora had stood and fought hard against her tears. "Patrick saved her," she admitted. Both Matt and Miranda were stunned by those words and Flora continued. "Miranda, Patrick came running and dove into the crashing waves. Anna was unconscious when he carried her to the shore. We got her resuscitated and he carried her to my house, but the cold… the wet… she took ill and never recovered. Her final words to me were to keep Patrick safe, and to never tell you what really happened to her. I don't think Patrick was ever aware that you didn't know. He would have told you what we couldn't bear to."

Matt was befuddled. Not having known about Patrick before these last few days, he had no idea he'd been there when Anna tried to take her own life.

Miranda slowly stood and went to the windows. She stared blankly out at the water and tried to absorb what she'd just heard. "It was because of her love for Seamus, wasn't it..." she breathed, barely above a whisper. She felt cold inside, sorrow for what her grandmother must have gone through.

Flora became angered and turned to Imogen. "And it was because of this unfeeling wretch of a woman," she said. "She drove her to do it." Flora was ready to finally release all of her true feelings, but Miranda stopped her.

"Wait... I want to hear everything," said Miranda. "Please, Miss Blackstone... tell me everything you told my grandmother."

Imogen raised her brows at Flora, and then turned her gaze to the young woman. "There's no turning back after you know everything," Imogen warned

"I'm already on the path of no return," said Miranda.

"All right," said Imogen. "What I am about to reveal to you, no one in this room knows but me. Until I told Anna, no one knew but me and my mother before me, and her father before her… And so on."

Miranda and the others listened very carefully to Imogen's words.

Imogen then raised her cane up and tapped it on the mantel above the fireplace. "What you need to do now, child, is open this book," Imogen instructed.

Miranda saw a very large, very old book on the mantel and picked it up. She blew the dust off of it and sat down next to Matt. There were no words on the cover. It was thick and the pages were uneven and seemed weathered. She opened it carefully.

"It's my family history," stated Imogen. "Start at the end… go on."

Miranda flipped through to the last page that had any writing. It was what amounted to a family tree. Her eyes grew large when she saw the last phrase written on the page. It read, '30 May 1944, Seamus Blackstone marries his true love, Alannah Mac Ceallach'.

Miranda read it aloud then quickly looked at Imogen.

"Yes," said Imogen. "That's your grandma's true name, as you know. And that was written by

Seamus well before the wedding. Two days before he was claimed by the horseman, in fact. He was a tad presumptuous."

"He was in love," Flora sternly corrected, barely holding back her disdain.

"Nevertheless," said Imogen. "The wedding never happened. Now go back a bit. A little bit closer to the beginning," she said. "Look for the year seventeen-sixty-seven, and the name Deóradháin Ó hAoileáin."

"As in Hyland?" Miranda resounded.

Matt and Flora were equally as surprised.

Imogen grinned. "Ah, yes. You wanted to know it all. Well, here it is."

Chapter Twenty-Five

ന്ദ്ര

Dorian Hyland

Matt took Miranda's hand between both of his to comfort her as they listened to all that Imogen had to say.

"It is said," began Imogen, "that nearly a thousand years ago an ancestor of mine was falsely accused of a murderous spree and beheaded under the ring of fire by his own kin. He rose from the grave, headless and fierce, on a great black steed and he cursed the family who betrayed him. He warned that now indeed the killing would begin, and that every Hyland son born under the ring of fire would share his fate.

'For centuries, the Hyland family was mindful of the curse and took every precaution to ensure a child would not be born under the ring of fire. The horseman would return each generation for his slaughter, but none were there to take his place. Eventually, the curse of the Hyland sons was all but forgotten and the fear of the horseman's vengeance was all that remained. But in seventeen-sixty-seven Deóradháin Ó hAoileáin was chosen.

'He was lord of the Castle Hyland which sat at the base of the Ballyroon. He was quite loved by all who knew him, and those who knew him well called him Dorian."

Miranda recalled the limerick she had read online and mouthed it aloud, 'Beware of Dorian Hyland…'"

Imogen finished for her, "'he rides at night 'til cold blood runs, a lot which will befall his sons… though lifetimes he may lie in wait, the ring of fire will seal their fate'. That too is in the book, Miranda. Turn the page. The poem is next to a copy of a painting which once hung in Dorian's castle."

Miranda did as she was told, and she saw the poem. But the painting truly caught her eye. She brushed her fingers over the picture delicately. It was of Dorian Hyland, and he was wearing the very same gold necklace that she now wore around her neck. She lifted the pendant and looked at it more closely.

"Dorian loved his wife, Órfhlaith, and she adored him, even worshipped him," Imogen explained. "The necklace was a gift from Órfhlaith to Dorian. Her initial is stamped on the front; a single phrase engraved on its back, 'mise go deo', yours forever. Dorian never took off the necklace, until it was thrust from his neck when he met with destiny. It is said that he visited his wife every night in his physical form, and on the night before the eclipse, he placed it around her neck and said, 'Wear this, and I shall know it is you'."

Flora knew this story was about to take a familiar turn and went to Miranda's side. She placed a supportive hand on her shoulder and looked to Imogen who stared knowingly at a doleful Miranda.

"This is the story as told to me and to my relatives before me. Órfhlaith watched as the horseman claimed her husband for the final time. Shadow riders appeared on black horses like a smoke from the ground and looked on as he was transformed into the vengeful dullahan. She was wrought with horror and screamed into the night as they disappeared.

'She waited for years in misery for his return. One night, the winds changed, and she felt him near. Every sensible person hid in their homes, locked their doors. But it wouldn't stop him. He found victims enough and Órfhlaith screamed as she watched. But she didn't run; she didn't hide from him. She chased him until he stopped on the road and turned around, finally taking heed to her pleas. He went to her and drew his sword as she knelt weeping in the mud. Unbeknownst to either of them, their son, Eamon, now grown, watched in disbelief from the roadside as his father climbed down from the horse and reached for her neck. He lifted the pendant from her chest and seemed to stare at it. She pulled herself up by his coat and cried to him. But he suddenly ripped the chain from her throat and threw it to the ground. He leapt back onto the horse and rode hard into the darkness.

'Eamon chased after his mother, but she ran into the sea and was lost forever. He believed that Órfhlaith thought the throwing away of the necklace meant that Dorian no longer loved her, but he felt it was the necklace that saved her from the sword. He kept the necklace which was passed through the generations until it went to Seamus.

'When the horseman comes to kill you can hear the cries of Órfhlaith, and of Clare, wife of Cian ó Braonáin, son of Rosaleen Hyland. And before long we'll hear–"

"Imogen!" yelled Flora. "Must we go on with this dramatic version of events?" She then turned to Miranda with a pleading stare.

Miranda did not hear Flora's question. Pain had once again pierced her heart, just as Flora had warned.

The wind began to howl and whip against the walls of the house. Imogen stood slowly with her cane and went with some eagerness to the windows. She looked as if she were watching for something. "It won't be long now," she remarked, a bit of elation in her voice. "But you'll have to make it through tonight first."

Matt had heard enough. He stood, his fists clenched tight, when Miranda intervened once again. She was winded by the story, humbled with the realization that all of the women before her had died in such misery. "Miss Blackstone," she said, "what about Seamus… and Patrick?" she asked.

Imogen turned around with cunning in her eyes. She looked at the girl and half-grinned. "Patrick, mm-hmm. I saw the look in your eyes when Flora told you he'd saved your grandma. What exactly is your relationship with Patrick?"

"That's not important," said Matt.

Imogen smirked. "Well, now I know, don't I?" she said smartly. She went closer to Miranda and the younger woman stood to meet her. They looked deliberately into each other's eyes and Miranda listened. She now knew that Patrick must be related to the Hylands Imogen spoke of but didn't understand just how. And she didn't know how Seamus was connected.

"My mother was Muireann Hyland," said Imogen. "She had a half-sister who was much younger than she. In fact, she was only three years younger than my brother Seamus. Her name was Maeve Hyland. She married Aonghus McShane, and bore only one child, a son, before dying in childbirth. He, like my brother, was born under the ring of fire. His name is Patrick Hyland McShane."

Miranda went away to the windows and opened one for the fresh air. The powerful wind blew through her hair and cooled her skin. Every single piece of this story was melding together, forming a clearer picture of Patrick's past. She wondered how much of it he knew.

Imogen continued as she returned to her seat. "My mother told me the history of the horseman but bade me never tell my brother. And neither of us ever did, until he was chosen."

Miranda turned around quickly. She was taken aback by those words. "You never told him?" A sickening feeling began to wash over her.

"Mother encouraged him to travel," said Imogen. "Looking back now, I think she was trying to spare him. But as you can see, he came back. It was as if he knew his destiny and had come to face it, although the horseman would have found him anywhere. There was no reason to tell him," Imogen coolly explained. "There was nothing to be done about it, and there's nothing to be done about it now."

Miranda's heart began to race. Everything Flora had said about this woman was true. She was callous and unfeeling. It was finally taking its toll. "There was no reason?" she echoed angrily.

"No," replied Imogen. "And if you've heard anything I've said since you got here, you'll realize that what will be, will be."

Miranda remembered hearing those words before, and Flora bit her lips feeling sorry she had said them the night she met Miranda.

Abruptly, Miranda ended the meeting. "Thank you for your time," she said disdainfully and then turned to exit.

"Take the book with you," said Imogen, as she stared into the fireplace. "Patrick and I are the only Hylands left in this family. My time's about up, and he's certainly never going to breed any heirs. Take it or leave it."

Flora and Matt were astonished by Imogen's final insufferable remark.

Miranda was speechless and so overwhelmed with feeling for Patrick that she refused to give this woman the satisfaction of a reaction. She took the book and headed for the door, but not before Imogen had one last word. The elderly woman stood and faced Miranda. "The only way to be with him is to join him in death," she drawled.

Flora dove in between the two; she was nearly nose to nose with Imogen. "Is that what you told Anna?" she blasted.

Imogen stared coldly. "She knew it was the truth," Imogen answered.

Matt quickly grabbed Flora, and with some difficulty assisted her from the house before her rage could erupt.

"Your suffering will come," Flora warned.

Emotionless, Imogen simply watched her be escorted away.

Chapter Twenty-Six

ɔ੪ഉ

A Plan

Riding back to Kilcrohane, Matt, Flora, and Miranda were silent. Meeting with Imogen had proved very enlightening, but nearly every word they'd heard pained them. Part of Miranda still clung to the hope of saving Patrick, but another part felt anguished, weak.

She held tight to the book Imogen had so willingly given to her and stared at it blankly as Matt drove the road along Dunmanus Bay. She flipped carefully through the book, and she could smell the oldness of it; the dusty, bittersweet scent permeated the rag paper pages and took her to another time and place. She read the words '…and for his trust he was paid with death, the Hylands and Cill Chrócháin shall never be the same'.

As the car came to a stop in front of Miranda's cottage, she had a sudden revelation. "How long will it take to get the town rallied together?" Miranda asked Matt.

He was dumbfounded and began to stammer. "The town? What? Why?"

"How long?" she repeated.

"Well… I don't know… with the horseman afoot, most folks aren't even leavin' their houses!"

Miranda put her hand on his shoulder. "The other night, after the horseman had gone, the men you were with said they would await further notice from you. It's time to give them that notice."

"I don't understand," said Matt.

"I want everyone you can possibly muster to meet me at Shivie's pub," she said.

"The pub?" echoed Flora. She was in shock. "What on earth do you want to go there for?" she asked.

Miranda took one last reckoning look at the book she held. "I want to try something;

something no one has tried before." Her eyes raised and gazed wholeheartedly into Matt's. "Please, Matt, tell me how long," she pleaded.

Matt swallowed hard and tried to understand. He didn't think anyone could be convinced to leave their homes, but her pleading eyes and desperate heart made him agree to try. "A few hours to do some convincing... if I'm lucky. O'Malley and Liam will go around too."

"And I'll help," said Flora.

"Thank you both," said Miranda. "Tell them that if they want to stop the horseman once and for all, they'll come and hear me out. I'll be there at six," she said.

Miranda paced the floor of the cottage, delicately touching every place that Patrick had touched; remembering every moment they'd shared. She breathed in the air still aware of his scent, the pleasing hint of wood spice; and the feel of the cool water on his skin as she'd nuzzled his neck after the rain. Memories of his voice, his understanding, his gentleness with her draped around her body like a comforting embrace. Her love for him burned inside her, not only as an eternal flame, but fueling her desire to save him from an evil fate. But she also realized something profound. Even if he could be saved from the curse what would become of him? Would he remain as he is, split between life and death—or would some other circumstance befall him? All she did know was that nothing could break their bond. And no matter what his fate would truly bring, she would be a part of it. Somehow, they would be together forever.

Six o'clock came faster than Miranda thought it would, and she chose to ignore how quickly the time now seemed to pass.

She left and began to drive down the road, the same dirt road where she'd witnessed the unthinkable. She looked in her rearview mirror to the place where she'd stood as the horseman reached for her. She grasped the pendant as she drove. Remembering that he'd pulled his hand away when she moved her hand from the necklace, she also recalled another memory. Anna had written over and over that he had known her name, but she didn't explain how she knew. If Eamon was right and the necklace was what spared his mother the sword, then maybe it all made sense. The horseman can indeed remember.

Miranda was starting to believe, whether by sensibility, or by desire, that the headless horseman was more than the tales gave him credit for. He was more than a ruthless, bloodthirsty, black rider. The men who became him were good men, they were deeply loved men. How could it be that they too shared his vengefulness?

Something began to play in Miranda's mind. If only the town would proclaim his innocence. Find a way to touch him deeply. Make him remember what started it all so he could make peace with it. Only light can vanquish darkness. We must bombard him with it. "I'm either a hopeless optimist or I've completely lost my mind," she said aloud. Then she shook her head, having realized that both observations were probably true.

She parked in front of the pub and no one seemed to be there. No other cars were in sight. But Miranda wasn't discouraged. She raised her head up and marched to the door, ever clinging to hope.

No one was inside except for an older gentleman who was wiping the tables with a dust cloth and straightening the chairs. "Well, hello there, young lady. Can I help ya' with somethin'?" he asked.

He seemed kindhearted, but a bit unnerved. His eyes shifted from Miranda to the door seemingly looking for someone to follow her inside.

"I was hoping to meet some people here," said Miranda. "They may be running a little late."

The man scoffed. "Won't come at all if they're smart," he said as he neared her. "Apparently, I'm not. Curiosity always gets the better of me. I suppose tonight might be the last time if I'm not careful." He then extended his hand to Miranda. "I'm Elliott. Pleased to meet you, Miss Kelly," he said knowingly. "Matthew has already been here."

Miranda smiled kindly at the man and shook his hand. She hoped everyone else would be this kind. If they showed up at all. "I'm pleased to meet you, sir."

Elliott suddenly looked behind her and a surprisingly large crowd of people began to pour inside the door.

Chapter Twenty-Seven

 CRISO

Gathering

The blanket of night fell upon Kilcrohane. The village outside was dark and quiet, but the small tavern was wild as the townsfolk discussed Miranda's idea and allowed her to plead her case. She begged them to listen, to consider the minute possibility of stopping the horseman, and without ever mentioning Patrick at all. But then, perhaps inevitably, the situation called for it.

Even as several people argued, some considering Miranda's plan and others refusing to hear of it, Miranda realized how close the people were to one another. She noticed that no matter how much they disagreed, they all wanted the same thing, to safeguard their town and each other. It was then that Miranda decided that after all these years, after decades of secrecy the truth had to be told. It was, quite possibly, her last hope of saving him. She stood firm and spoke loud and clear. "Patrick Hyland McShane lives."

The room became silent at once. Matt and O'Malley shared looks of shock because of Miranda's blatant statement. The other people, four women and seventeen men, stared directly at Miranda for an explanation. Not a single soul uttered a word. No one could believe what they'd just heard Miranda proclaim.

They stared on as O'Malley marched up beside her, his head a little higher than it had ever been. "She's tellin' the truth!" said O'Malley, his eyes firmly on those of Liam, who had questioned his sanity on many occasions. "Tell'em, Miranda!"

"Now, wait a minute," said Liam. He stood tall and broad, his hair was dusty blonde, his face weathered from a life of good hard work. He turned his eyes to Miranda's. "We already know about the horseman. It's been our town secret for many an age," he said in a deep tone. "But are you trying to tell us that O'Malley is right, and

Patrick's ghost has been wandering around here too for all these years?"

"Why haven't we seen him?" asked Elliott. "Forty-some years is a long time!"

"I've seen him," said a woman. Her eyes were on the floor as she sat and she spoke barely above her breath, but everyone heard her. "At least I think I have," she said. "Years ago, I remember going for a stroll, a bit later than I had before—or since. I saw someone else walking in the dark, but he didn't seem to notice me. I wondered who else would be out that late, and when the moon hit him just right, I could have sworn... Well, I never told a soul because I knew you'd think I was as mad as O'Malley."

"Well!" said O'Malley. "Doesn't that beat all?" he huffed, folding his arms.

Another large man stood up and sighed. "I've seen him too," he said.

O'Malley's eyes grew large. He was just about to the breaking point when several other people confessed to having thought they'd seen Patrick and denied it to themselves. O'Malley's mouth was two inches from the floor, but Miranda felt more at ease. She began to explain the entire sordid story as quickly and as completely as she could. Most of the townspeople seemed to understand, but many still questioned her plan to try and stop the horseman. The risk was great and the chance for survival was low. Without her confessing her love for Patrick, it was still clear to them why she was doing all of this. They felt for her, but that wouldn't save their necks.

The hour was getting nearer, and Miranda worried that they would not be willing to take such a risk. But she questioned herself, who am I to ask them to?

Unexpectedly, Flora entered the pub and all eyes fell on her. Earlier, she told Miranda she would help, but hadn't said just how. She'd gone to investigate something and felt she needed to share what she discovered with the people of Kilcrohane.

The villagers seemed less tense than they usually had been around Flora, but she knew this was due to Miranda's story, which she'd heard from outside the open door. She grinned slyly and went to the younger woman. "You should go, Miranda. You're work here is done. Spend what time you can with him." Flora's words were veritable, but difficult to hear. It could truly be

Miranda's last night with Patrick Hyland McShane.

Suddenly, a loud and long piercing scream stopped the hearts of everyone in the tavern. It sent a painful shrill up Miranda's spine. This was a scream the likes of which she had never heard.

"It's a siren!" someone exclaimed. "A banshee! The horseman is here!"

Everyone clambered to cut the lights and close and barricade the door.

"He couldn't wait until tomorrow!" someone yelled.

"He's after one last taste of blood!" said another.

Miranda began to panic that the horseman had come early for Patrick. "Let me through!" screamed Miranda, plowing through the crowd in the dark to get to the door.

"Have you lost your mind, girl?" called Matt. He and O'Malley couldn't see Miranda, but they forced their way to the door to help block her in. No one noticed her open a window and climb out until it was too late. She ran to her car, but the keys were still inside in her purse. She had no choice but to run home instead.

Chapter Twenty-Eight

ርፄନ

A Scream in the Night

Miranda ran down the middle of the road, but she was not alone. She heard footsteps on the ground behind her and she turned to see that several men from the pub were coming after her. The others had gathered outside the door of Shivie's and looked on. But she didn't stop, until the screaming began again. It was the horrific wail of a woman.

The cry was long and wrought with misery. Only the word 'no' could be distinguished.

Miranda and the men were halted in their tracks. The lone scream seemed to envelope the town. It came from the north, the south, everywhere. Then all at once, it became silent. Flora stepped out in front of the men and paused.

Out of the shadows ahead of Miranda stepped a familiar and shocking sight. It was the elderly and ostensibly wicked, Imogen Blackstone. She eked her way from the side of the road with her cane and went up to Miranda.

"How did you get here?" asked Miranda worriedly.

"Don't you worry about that," said Imogen. "I get where I need to be, when I need to be there."

"You need to get out of here!" Miranda exclaimed. "The horseman–"

"I heard Anna's screams," said Imogen. "I know he's here."

"Anna's?" Miranda echoed.

"It must be," said Imogen. "It's her Seamus who's riding the night, bent on killing."

Miranda was stammered. Her own grandmother… could that have been her voice? That troubled, anguished voice… Miranda clutched her chest.

"Do you still think you can save my cousin?" Imogen asked. "Do you think you won't end up like Anna, and all of the countless women in my family before her who once thought like you?"

Her voice was firm and as cruel as possible. She stared purposefully into Miranda's eyes.

"Would you be willing to look straight at the devil and say, you're not taking that man from me?"

Miranda forcefully uttered only one word. "Yes."

"That's all I needed to hear," said Imogen.

Miranda was taken aback by that remark, but she didn't have time to respond, for Imogen began again quickly.

"There is a way to break the curse," stated Imogen. "None before you were strong enough, but you... you might be able to do it. You'll only have one chance. I tell you this before I die because, for the first time, I think there might be hope."

The sound of hooves heavily pounding the ground could suddenly be heard. Miranda tried to grab Imogen and help her to safety, but the old woman stood firm. "Miranda Kelly," Imogen began, "when the sun and moon align, the horseman will take Patrick's head, there won't be any stopping it," she said.

"You're wrong–" Miranda began and tried again to move Imogen, but she was cut off and Imogen dropped her cane and grabbed Miranda's arms.

"Hear me!" cried Imogen. "Patrick cannot appear by day, but he *will* appear in the darkness under the ring of fire, noon tomorrow, and the horseman will take him. You must be prepared. Patrick will be consumed with power, his ethereal body and what's left of his physical one will join—"

The thumping of the hooves could now be felt. The horseman drew very near. Imogen spoke as fast as she could. "Listen to me! Patrick will become the headless horseman and the shadow riders will rise from the earth to claim the head! This will seal the fate of his soul forever!""

Miranda saw the black horse appear. It stood, menacingly on the road beyond the elderly woman. Its rider held tight to the reigns and loomed toward the two women. Miranda was frozen in time once more.

Imogen did not turn around to see what she knew was coming. "Miranda," said Imogen, for the first time with warmth in her voice. "You must make Patrick remember you before the shadow riders come. If they come for him, it will be too late." Imogen then straightened her posture and smiled, knowing the horseman was close behind her.

As the others watched in horror, most from the windows, Miranda backed away, her eyes fixed on the dullahan clad in black leather as he slid the sword from its sheath. The horseman had slowed his horse to a labored walk and made way slowly toward the two women.

"Imogen… come… come away," Miranda stuttered. The smell of blood on the cool wind permeated the air as he drew closer.

Imogen smiled contentedly, her back ever turned to the horseman. And then she closed her eyes with a smile and whispered softly, "I am ready, Seamus."

With one fast whip of his sword, Imogen's neck cleanly left her shoulders.

Miranda fell backward onto the hard, wet ground. She was horrified and shocked. Her heart was stilled.

The horseman's steed stepped beside her. The black horse snarled, and its searing breath was patently visible on the cold night air. The horseman lowered his bloody sword to Miranda's chin and, with the point of it, lifted the chain from around her neck. With a flick of his wrist, he ripped it from her throat, and climbed down from his horse.

With vehement authority, Patrick roared, "Don't you touch her!" He bolted to Miranda and shoved the horseman hard, but the sinister dullahan was unmoved.

Both Patrick and the horseman were of equally large size, and they now met for the first time, shoulder to shoulder. But the horseman's strength was inhuman. He grabbed Patrick by the throat with tremendous power and pulled him closer. With his other hand he placed the blade of his sword against the flesh of Patrick's neck and sliced him, slowly, deliberately.

Patrick began to heave as the blood streamed down his neck, and he clenched his teeth hard in anger, but did not wince.

Gripping Patrick's neck tighter so the blood would flow harder, the horseman raised his arm and pointed his blade to the dark sky above where the new moon would soon meet the sun.

"No!" Miranda cried. She rushed to Patrick as the horseman threw him to the ground.

After snatching up the head of Imogen Blackstone, the horseman angrily leapt back onto his horse. Somehow, the sinister guffaw of the dullahan could be heard as he rode fast down the foggy rode and disappeared.

Chapter Twenty-Nine

ႢႩႬ

Comfortably Numb

Miranda held Patrick and watched in horror as the blood flowed from his neck. She tore open his bloodied shirt and saw the streams of blood flow down his chest. "Patrick!" she cried. "Tell me you're all right!"

But Patrick's rage at the dullahan had left as quickly as it had risen. The feeling of surrender overcame him once more. It was a feeling he'd felt for many years; the realization that he could not change his destiny. It was an acceptance that had left him comfortably numb for all these years. That was, until Miranda Kelly entered his life.

Miranda. Her touch on his skin had brought him back to his senses. He had not even heard her screaming his name. But the feeling that emanated from her fingertips surged through him and woke him from his trance-like state. He stared deep into her tear-filled eyes. "Miss Kelly," he breathed, "I don't want this for you."

"Patrick," said Miranda, "I don't want this for you either, but at least we're together."

Patrick climbed to his feet and Miranda held him close. But suddenly Patrick's eyes rose, and he became instantly aware that they were not alone. In his haste to protect Miranda from the horseman, he had rushed out of the shadows and into the startled view of a growing crowd.

He'd been revealed, exposed. And, to his extreme disbelief, as they laid their eyes upon him for the first time in over forty years, they didn't seem startled, rather relieved. They leaned on one another, some embraced, and each stared on at him compassionately.

Patrick looked down into Miranda's gracious eyes. He was overwhelmed and hoping she would have an answer.

"I will explain," she said sweetly, softly. "But first, let's go home."

Flora stared at Patrick for several moments from a distance and then she ushered the crowd inside as Patrick and Miranda walked away slowly down the dark road.

Patrick sat in a chair in Miranda's cottage and stared outward into the night. He seemed despondent and was silent. Miranda was unsure whether any thoughts went through his mind or whether he was simply overwhelmed with them. She'd told him the story that Imogen had told, and she showed him the book of his family history. He now knew why he was chosen, and he was further convinced that this was truly his destiny. He hadn't had much to say, and Miranda didn't press him for his thoughts.

Miranda heard what sounded like a car pulling up. She peeked through the door and saw what looked like two people riding away in Matt's truck. They had dropped off her car and hadn't wanted to bother her. She was grateful for both gestures and hurriedly returned to Patrick.

She cleaned his bloody skin with a cool damp cloth and was surprised to find that the wound was gone. It had disappeared. She traced his neck with her fingertips. "Patrick…" she mouthed. "It's gone. How?"

Patrick simply closed his eyes. He didn't say a word. Miranda knew the truth in her heart. Patrick truly had been doomed to live on all these years, waiting for the inevitable. He could not die until it was time. She would say nothing more. Instead, she placed her palm soothingly against one side of his face and gently kissed him on the other. He took her by the wrist to halt her just after the kiss and looked lovingly into her eyes. "There's a place I want to take you," he said.

She kissed his lips softly and said, "Yes, anywhere."

Patrick stood and took Miranda's sweater from the hook and wrapped it around her shoulders. His every move was slow, deliberate. He paid careful attention to every detail of her face, her hair. He looked forlorn, and yet truly in love. Miranda knew he was beginning to say goodbye. Her heart suddenly felt hollow, alone, but she fought it with every ounce of her being. And she said nothing. She let him guide her to wherever he would take her.

Chapter Thirty

⟨⟩

Perfect Love

Now under the phase of the new moon, the land was dark. Miranda drove with Patrick at her side and he directed her to a secluded place.

They left the car, and he took her by the hand. He led her to a small hidden cove. It was dark without the light of the moon, but the blanket of bright stars above could be seen twinkling in the clear water before them. As her eyes adjusted to the night, Miranda could make out a waterfall pouring gracefully over the rocks and the pleasing scent of thistle and wild orchids permeated the cool night air.

Patrick slid his hand across Miranda's neck and gently traced her chin with his thumb. He then pulled her close and kissed her waiting lips. He breathed her in… filled himself with her essence. This kiss was a mark of the depth of their love. It was deep. It was pure. It was forever.

Still holding each other, his forehead gently fixed against hers, Patrick uttered his words so passionately, so fervidly that it created a resonance that would live a lifetime within her. "I love you," he said.

Time stood still for Miranda. She had to catch her breath. The love they shared was inherent, but she'd only just realized he had never said the words to her before. And when he'd said them, so much more than love was in his voice.

"I love you," she replied. And that instant she knew she had never meant anything more in her life.

Their wanting lips met once more, and Patrick removed the sweater from Miranda's shoulders. He unbuttoned her shirt, slowly. And she unbuttoned his. The chill of the night air seemed absent as their body heat began to rise.

Fully removed of their clothing, Miranda stood against him, and Patrick pressed her closer by the small of her back. He moved his mouth to her cheek, her ear, her neck. Miranda began to quietly moan, but Patrick slid his hand down her arm and took her by the hand. "Come into the water," he whispered.

Expectedly, Miranda winced at the thought of the potential coldness of the water. But Patrick soothed her with his words. "Trust me," he said softly. And all her reservations disappeared.

Patrick led Miranda slowly into the water and she was very surprised to find the water was not cold, but cool. She stepped all the way in, her faith solely in his hands.

"It's a hot spring," said Patrick.

"In Ireland?" Miranda queried with a grin.

"There are a few," Patrick answered.

"How did you find it?" asked Miranda.

Patrick pulled her close to him and paused before he answered. "I've had a lot of time on my hands," he said calmly.

Miranda was tossed fervently back into reality. Her mouth agape, words of trepidation trying to escape, Patrick hushed her with a whisper. "Don't talk," he said, "just feel."

"But, Patrick, we're running out of–" She tried to speak, and the presence of tears were beginning to sting her eyes.

"Don't talk," he repeated. "Don't think…"

He stroked her hair and kissed her head, and then she laid it upon his chest and tried with all of her will to live in this moment, to do as he'd asked.

The couple swam in the water, frolicking, embracing. Soon Miranda's eyes were fully acclimated to the darkness and the light of the stars seemed as bright as dusk. She realized it was the reason Patrick could see so well at night, something she noted that night in the woods when he'd led her to the little red bridge. He'd lived by night for so many years, he'd become one with it.

And she'd become one with it as well, only able to hold him at night, speak to him at night. She tried not to wonder what life would be like if the horseman succeeded. But what would happen if he did not? She'd never pondered that before. If the curse could be broken, what would become of Patrick? He was supposed to have died all those years ago. If the horseman was stopped, would Patrick stay as he is, or would he vanish from this earth forever?

Miranda halted in the water. Anxiety and confusion began to reclaim her. She'd never thought it completely through. Was there truly no possibility for a happy ending? She'd been warned so many times…

Suddenly, Patrick took her by the arms and tried to steal her gaze. "I told you not to think…" he reminded calmly.

Miranda truly was speechless. She'd just been struck by a thunderbolt. Maybe this was it. Maybe this truly was their last night together, their last time together, forever.

Miranda looked up into Patrick's silent eyes. And she connected with him on an awakened level. No words were necessary or could even be said. For the first time, Miranda fully realized the scope of this condition. What she had never allowed herself to believe had become true. She now understood how Patrick had accepted that what would happen would happen… one way or another.

She stood in the water in silence. The tips of her soaking wet tresses drifted carelessly in the water; tears fell silently, freely from her eyes.

"It's okay for me to go," Patrick suddenly admitted.

Miranda was partly shaken from her thoughts when he said this.

"Because of your love, my heart will always be at peace," said Patrick. "I am not afraid."

Miranda felt herself exhale. Inside, her heart began to weep. She reached up and stroked his wet hair; it was slick and darkened by the tepid water.

It was her turn to memorize his features. Unconsciously, she noted the boldness of his jawline, the tenderness of his lips, and the gentle emerald eyes that loved her an eternity with just a glance.

Patrick lifted Miranda and her legs entwined effortlessly around him. He slowly led her behind the gentle waterfall. The taste of the water on his lips and the scent on his skin intoxicated her, soothed her.

Both were overcome with love and emotion. Their feelings had reached a height of such intensity that both were now blind to all but their passion.

Patrick carefully placed Miranda on a smooth stone platform that was covered in soft Irish moss. And for the rest of the night, they made perfect love amongst the gentle sprays and tranquil song of the magical falls.

Chapter Thirty-One

❧

Eclipse

Patrick had said his goodbyes, without words. When Miranda awoke, dawn had long since passed and she was in her bed alone. When she realized this, she sat up suddenly and gasped for breath.

The sun was bright and filled her room as it had no other day since she arrived. The splendor of it taunted her, cruelly implying that it would be a pleasing, joyful day.

She was immediately struck with unease over Patrick's tribulation. The hour was near that could remove him of all he knew forever. She felt poisoned; a sickness began to stir within her core, but she fought hard against it. The sun was high and at any moment the eclipse would begin. Patrick would appear during the day for the first time in over forty years. And she would be there to see him; she would be there to hold him; she would be there to stop this madness no matter what dangers she faced.

As Miranda dressed, the new moon began to subtly mute the light of the relentless sun by cooling its burning western edge. She left her hair down and natural and wore no cosmetics of any kind. She looked over the gold medallion hard, one last time, before slipping it over her head and under her hair.

Her head high, she opened the door and left the small cottage, taking nothing else with her. She left the door open, her keys and bag on the table. She took nothing but limitless devotion and courage and began to walk to the center of town. She knew that Patrick would appear there. She knew that his resolve and valor would lead him to march to the center of it all, to face his destiny head-on, and so would she.

As Miranda neared the village, the scents of herbs and newly blossoming flowers brought to mind the time she'd spent with Patrick; talks of planting, walking in the woods. And the cool, moist breeze that rolled in from the shore reminded her of dancing in the rain and making love under the soothing waterfall. Yet, the fading sun caught her eye and reminded her how he'd disappeared like a wisp of golden dust in the wind, and how the ring of fire threatened to take him permanently into another existence.

But an unexpected sound called Miranda's attention. She could hear deep voices on the wind as if in song. The sound came from nearby. Getting closer to the village, Miranda saw the townspeople grouped together, some seated, some standing. Matt and O'Malley were nearest to her, and every person lent his voice to what was a profound and tranquil song of the sea.

A young Old Man as wild as the sea
Cooled the red horizon with his frigid stare
Into the tempest he led us, salt like her blood
O'er the boundary, against the terrible swell
His heart was a ballast, kept us steady and sound
Fearless and stubborn, his dignity stout
Our reverence of the Captain, time cannot wane
In our ancient hearts the muse of his mettle remains

Miranda knew immediately that they too understood what the darkness would bring, and that Patrick would boldly come to the center of it all to meet it. They too would set aside their fears and face the evil that threatened him.

As they soulfully sang the last words of the song, those who were sitting stood up and next to their friends, and all observed the darkening sky. The moon moved slowly but deliberately across the sun. The ring of fire was nearly in view.

Matt and O'Malley stood by Miranda's side. Matt held a reassuring hand at her back, partly in support of her and partly for himself.

As the black moon took its place in the center of the sun, a burning ring of fire became all at once present like a beacon warning those below. The time had come.

The breeze was suddenly an icy embrace. The land became dark, and Miranda, ever still, gazed around anxiously for Patrick to appear. She clasped the medallion hard and listened for even the faintest sound. The people of Kilcrohane crowded together. Their senses were also heightened as they waited in the dark for any sign of Patrick, or of anyone else.

Suddenly, the town was engulfed in a familiar and unnatural silence. A light fog began to roll forth across the land that separated them from the sea. The sky was suddenly streaked with emerald light which seemed to emanate from the black horizon. The ring of fire burning brightly above, the ground began to rumble lowly, deliberately. It was as if the earth was quietly breaking apart. But soon the rumble faded. And there, in the far distance, was the black silhouette of the horseman on his steed. Behind him, the brilliant green ribbons of aurora borealis charged the darkened sky. But the horseman was not alone.

Imogen's now immortal words rang loud in Miranda's ears, 'You must make Patrick remember you before the shadow riders come. If they come for him, it will be too late.' But before Miranda's anguished eyes she could clearly see that the riders had already come.

Miranda stepped forward onto the road and saw clearly that several black figures on horses were lined up on either side of the headless horseman. But they were not headless; and together they were an unquestionably dominating presence.

The horseman drew his sword, and a fell whisper could be heard, seemingly from everywhere. "Patrick Hyland McShane, your time has come."

The townspeople were more afraid than ever, yet they stood strong and steadfast against whatever they would have to face.

Miranda ran several steps up the roadway toward the horseman and Matt and O'Malley were unable to grab her. "Patrick!" she yelled. Her voice was strained with worry and pain as she waited frantically for him to arrive.

And, like a star first appearing in the clear night sky, Patrick slowly appeared. He stood a short distance from Miranda, nearer to her than to the horseman, but the vile dullahan was quickly fixed on Patrick's presence. He began to press forward.

Miranda ran to Patrick, who stood ever still. He stared at her as she got closer. His benevolent heart was filled with pain. He knew the horseman was nearing behind him. He knew that this was truly the end. He looked at the medallion around Miranda's neck and then deep into her terrified and love-filled eyes one last time. "Mise go deo," he breathed before turning away.

Then, the terrified but courageous townspeople ran up the roadway screaming, shouting, foregoing fear in a valiant effort to distract the horseman. But the murderous beast was unfazed by the commotion. He rode hard and fast, eagerly to his successor. But the people were determined as well and ran even harder. They rushed between Patrick and the vigilant horseman, and risking their lives, they stood boldly against him.

"Bombard him with light," Miranda whispered.

As was their plan, the people shouted in unison a statement that dazed the horseman. "Deaglán Ó hAoileáin, gur fear neamhchiontach thú! Declan O'Hyland, you are an innocent man!"

The horseman, perhaps caught off guard by those words, yanked hard on the reigns and his furious steed reared upward, its hind legs sliding roughly on the rocky roadway and knocking a few townsmen violently to the ground. The wild horse spun full circle and the horseman tightened his hold. He seemed bowled over, but whether it was due to the proclamation of innocence, or the hearing of his name for the first time in a thousand years, no one could be certain.

Miranda and the other villagers had hoped that those words would speak to the heart of the man who once lived. If they could at last give him redemption, a modicum of relief from his torment might at last be felt, however small or brief. But the horseman quickly regained control.

Holding his sword high, he returned his focus to Patrick, who readily faced him. Patrick's eyes were fixed on the headless rider in black and his portentous steed whose seething, blood-imbued breath now warmed his face.

Miranda quickly grabbed Patrick by the arm and tried to pull him away, but Patrick was unmoved. Time seemed to slow as the townspeople once again tried to delve between Patrick and the horseman, risking the dullahan's rising blade. Some pleaded and cried, others shouted again and again, in Declan's ancient tongue and in their own, words of peace, forgiveness, and of his innocence. Once again, the horseman seemed affected. And this time, he backed his horse away from the crowd.

Before arriving at the pub, the night before, Flora had acted on a feeling based on something Imogen had said. She'd said that the Hyland curse had begun centuries ago. Flora then remembered a book on her own shelf that told of the legend of Declan O'Hyland, the noble man who was unjustly beheaded for crimes he had not committed. After his curse on the family, the real murderer was discovered. But the revelation had come too late for Declan. The legend also told of the shadow riders. It said that the headless horseman is driven by the resentment that all prior horsemen felt for being taken from their loved ones and by what the first horseman felt for being wrongfully beheaded. He can feel these emotions and knows not why. But he finds relief when he is freed from the confines of that body. When his successor takes his place, he leaves his emotions behind, and his shadow moves on to become one of the hapless, black souls known as the shadow riders.

The shadow riders see to it that the new horseman takes his place, then immediately after, they take his head into the depths to seal his fate forever.

Flora now believed that the body of the horseman still held the emotional spirit of every Hyland son who'd ever become the horseman, beginning with the first. When she heard Miranda pleading a case to the villagers that declaring his innocence might stop him, Flora immediately considered the possibility. If such a meaningful declaration from the entire town might be strong enough to break through, even for an instant… to make him remember, to make him feel something other than rage. She didn't know what would happen, if anything, or whether it could help Patrick, but they had to try. She'd told the townspeople Declan's name and to follow through with Miranda's plan, but she didn't tell them that she had an additional plan at work.

Miranda's screams were unheard by Patrick, who broke free from her grasp and moved forward pushing the people aside as he made his way to the horseman. He would not let anyone else be harmed in a futile attempt to save him. The horseman, who was temporarily caught off guard, refocused once again and jumped down from his horse, blade in hand.

The two men forcefully walked toward each other as if straight into battle. Patrick could hear nothing clearly but what he knew to be the final pounds of his heart.

The shadow riders began to descend and soon surrounded the headless horseman and Patrick, forcing Miranda and the villagers away.

They rode in a circle around the two, in a stalking manner, the scent of leather, smoke, and ash permeated the cool air. The moon was slowly moving across the sun, and the horseman was losing time.

But Flora Farrelly appeared on a nearby glade, amongst the grassy mounds on the landscape. Her zealous voice carried on the wind. "Horseman hear me! You shall not take this man!"

Her call was met with no response. With outstretched arms she spoke low as if she were conversing secretly with the wind. Eyes closed and palms to the sky, she spoke with utter intensity. "Perfect light shall free your soul."

A white light appeared before her and slowly took the shape of a woman. As the figure moved forward her image became clearer. Miranda looked her way in bewilderment. Before her eyes was her grandmother, Anna Kelly.

The older woman remained somewhat translucent as she neared the horseman. She appeared younger, healthier than even Miranda remembered. And her eyes were set on the headless dullahan.

"Seamus Blackstone," said Anna softly, with pure love in her voice. "Come to me. Harm no one. Come to me, Seamus."

The horseman did not heed her. He was furious as he stormed the ground. His black cape flailing behind him in the wind, he took his sword into both of his gloved hands and raised it above him.

Just as he reached Patrick, the spirit of Anna Kelly approached as well, and she walked slowly through the headless horseman, filling his fierce body with her essence, then she vanished. He stopped abruptly and stood still, clearly affected by her presence. But the shadow riders reared their horses and then quickly closed in more forcefully on the horseman.

Miranda had no doubt that he felt Anna and remembered her—but in an instant he returned to his merciless purpose. He whipped the sword above him twice.

Patrick refused to even blink his eyes as the horseman swung one last time and then mercilessly thrashed his blade cleanly across Patrick's neck. Patrick dropped to his knees before the horseman, his head still attached until he fell completely to the ground.

Horrorstruck, Miranda ran carelessly through the ring of riders and directly to Patrick's headless, lifeless body.

A terrible lightning filled the sky and the horseman suddenly dropped his sword, sending it clanking to the ground. His arms outstretched, a golden current surged from Patrick's body to his. The horseman's body seemed to writhe with pain and began to yell in agony.

Miranda, untouched by the surge, turned Patrick to his back and held onto him. She refused to let go. Her anguished screams and pleads for this to end were ignored and even relished by the riders surrounding her.

But suddenly, the horseman faded into shadow and then to nothingness, and, while still in her embrace Patrick's body began to transform into a familiar and foreboding semblance of what she once knew. He now wore black leather armor over his chest, and all black clothing neck to foot with tall buckled boots and a textured leather cape as the horseman had worn. Miranda was speechless. She could scarcely breathe. Patrick had become the headless horseman.

"Get out of there, Miranda!" yelled Matt, desperately.

"Hurry, girl! Please!" O'Malley shouted.

The other townspeople joined in with similar cries, but it all fell on deaf ears, for still she would not leave him. They screamed, yet she heard nothing.

"Patrick, please!" she began to lament, over and over.

Then, as if having been filled with a cleansing breath of life, Patrick's body began to move. First, with a strong left hand, he gripped Miranda's wrist. She froze and waited for what he might do to her, but not in fear.

He let go of her and then began to stand. Miranda, still on the ground, looked upward at the towering frame which stood before her. He looked even stronger, more massive than before. Without thought, she grabbed onto his leg and pleaded, "Please know me. Patrick, please know me—"

Patrick slowly bent down, nearing Miranda's tear-drenched face; and as she felt hope flicker in her heart, he picked up the sword from beside her and brought it gingerly past her neck as he returned to a straight position.

She stood and screamed at him, "Fight it! Patrick, fight against it! Remember me! Remember the medallion!"

But he pushed her aside and turned to his horse. He placed his sword in its sheath and walked steadfast and with purpose, taking no heed to her pleas.

The shadow riders began to move once more, and one neared the new horseman's head which still lay on the ground. He would take it to the searing depths in order to seal the new horsemen's fate.

Miranda chased after Patrick and continued to plead. As he reached the black horse, she grabbed him once more and he turned swiftly around. The headless horseman stood coldly before her. He was threatening, dangerous, and a frightening presence to all others who watched, but to Miranda, he was Patrick, her true love no matter his form.

"Fight this, Patrick, please!" she cried. She wept hard into his chest, the taste of his leather on her lips. "I love you," she uttered wearily. "I love you."

Without warning, he took her by the throat and held her out at arm's length. Her eyes grew large and she gasped for air. He did not choke her but held her firmly and still and almost lifted her from the ground.

Matt and O'Malley wanted to rush to her aid, but Flora abruptly stopped them.

"No!" she said. "You must wait…"

As Patrick held Miranda she cried with effort, "Patrick, I love you…"

His grip on her loosened, but only slightly.

Then, just as one of the shadow riders took up Patrick's head from the ground, a chorus of feminine voices could be heard singing a beautiful melody. The voices were getting louder and nearer with each passing second. The shadow riders became anxious. They backed up, their horses began to stir and whimper as the presence loomed forward.

It was countless singing women in white. They were transparent, but vibrant, and surrounded by a delicate white light which was an ethereal mist. As the women sang in an ancient Irish tongue, they surrounded the shadow riders and forced them within their own ghostly circle. They were the banshees. They were the spirits of the horsemen's loves. They were Órfhlaith, Clare, and many others.

Patrick suddenly let go of Miranda. The shadow riders, fearful of the ghostly ladies in white and of the strength and love they embodied, faded down into the ground from whence they came, leaving something quite valuable behind.

The peaceful song of the banshees quieted to a soft hum and a soothing wind began to swirl around Miranda and Patrick. The banshees circled the young couple and held hands as they continued their melody. It was a song of remembrance and love.

Miranda took hold of Patrick and he began to tremble. Something was happening to him.

The banshees continued their song as Miranda held Patrick tight. Soon, a brilliant light began to emanate from his body, and he abruptly fell to his knees. Miranda stood back. Bright orbs began to emerge from that light and to take the shapes of his Hyland kin—the men who'd been cursed as the horsemen before him. Peacefulness surrounded them as the men appeared one by one and were at once reunited with their long-lost loves.

But suddenly, the emanating light became a dense and powerful mist that poured across the ground and then rose into the figure of a man. He was tall and fierce-looking, and as he neared, he became lighter as if to turn from shadow into perfect light. He walked deliberately by the people of Kilcrohane and looked meaningfully into the eyes of each man and woman. When he approached Miranda, he took one of her hands into his own and stared deep into her eyes. She did not know his face, but immediately knew who he was. He was Declan O'Hyland. And he said to her the words he meant for the entire town, but with a sentiment in his voice that told her he had felt the love she had bestowed on Patrick even while he was the horseman. "Go raibh maith agat," he said. In her heart she understood his words were 'thank you'. Miranda was breathless.

Patrick began to stand, and Miranda grabbed hold of him with her other hand, ever heedless of any perils that might impose. He seemed to steady himself and then his body seemed to relax.

Declan, still holding Miranda's hand, gripped her hand tighter. She turned to him in time to catch a soothing smile, and then he faded before her eyes.

The otherworldly haze followed, and as it did, the benevolent spirit of Seamus Blackstone appeared in his spectral and healthy form. Then

Anna reappeared at his side. She went at once to her granddaughter. The two women stared deep into each other's eyes, instantly reliving the flood of memories they'd shared and speaking their love for each other in silence. Anna stroked her granddaughter's cheek, and to Miranda her skin felt cool and gentle as she'd always remembered. Anna spoke only one sentence before parting. "It'll be all right." Then she took Seamus by the arm and they drifted slowly into the night with the other spirits. The centuries of torturous heartache seemed vanquished in an instant.

Miranda immediately took Patrick's hand and removed the glove. He stood ever still. His hand was just as she knew it to be, strong but gentle, and unchanged. She kissed his palm and placed it lovingly against her cheek. "Patrick," she said through tears, her voice broken. "It's your Miss Kelly… It's your Miss Kelly."

With those words, Miranda felt something come alive in him and she knew with her heart and soul that he remembered her. She held him tightly in her arms and again began to profess her love. He suddenly slid his arms around her and held her back as tightly as he ever had. It was absolute confirmation that he remembered her and loved her still. At last she was filled with hope and elation.

But the moon slipped away, and the sun came into full view. As it shined down on the embracing couple below, Patrick began to vanish as he had every morning for forty-three years.

"No!" Miranda cried. "It can't be! Don't leave me! Patrick!"

And for the last time, the shimmering particles of light that was her Patrick fell upon her and vanished. Every trace of his physical body was gone. This time, however, his voice could be heard as it was carried gently on the breeze, "Your love has given me peace."

Miranda collapsed, unable to utter a single word. She was weak, heartbroken, and rapidly dying inside. Words could not be said to tell of her grief. She wearily clutched the dirt and rock and wept wholeheartedly onto the cold ground. The grief-stricken people of Kilcrohane could do nothing but deeply mourn.

Chapter Thirty-Two

ᏣᏋᏏᎧ

Sunlight

Many days passed and Miranda, crestfallen, could
do little more than lie in bed or stare through the
window. She was sick with anguish and the
support of her troubled friends could do nothing
to console her.

On this day, the sun was no longer eclipsed
by the moon, but by the clouds of the darkening
sky. Thunder rumbled low, but Miranda could not
hear it. The flowers were growing fuller, more
fragrant, but Miranda took no notice.

She climbed out of bed where she'd laid
clothed and silent, slipped on her shoes, and went
outside for the first time since the eclipse. She

walked straight across the road to where she'd sat looking at the sea on the night she'd met Patrick. She leaned against the tree there and looked out at the rich blue water. She remembered her first meeting with Patrick, the way he smiled when she'd been startled, the gentlemanly way he'd helped her to her feet, and the way he'd softly kissed her hand. From the start he made her feel new, beautiful, loved. She smiled to herself for the first time in a long time.

Then the sky suddenly began to clear. The thunder and clouds faded away and the sun gently lit up the earth. Miranda turned to gaze down the road hoping to see Patrick walking toward her one last time. The pain returned to her heart when she saw nothing but the road ahead…

But suddenly, she saw movement in the sunlight. She thought she saw a person walking up the road, but instantly knew it was the affects of a cruelly wishful mind. She wanted him so badly her wishes were beginning to materialize.

She turned back to the water but couldn't raise her eyes to see it. She fell to her knees next to the tree. Pained, she began to weep once more.

But this time, someone took her gently by the shoulder. "Don't cry, Miss Kelly," he said.

Miranda became quiet and slowly opened her eyes. She couldn't bear another hallucination. She reluctantly turned and looked into the eyes of the man kneeling next to her. It was Patrick. And he was just as she knew him, in his perfect human form. "It isn't you," she cried. "This isn't real..."

Patrick smiled and took her face into his hands. "It is real," he said. "I am here, and I'm not going anywhere for a very long time. You saved me, Miranda. You stopped the shadow riders from completing their task—from taking my head. When they left it behind, the curse was broken and the spirits of the horsemen before me were freed. Love and light drove the darkness away."

Gently, he brushed the tears from her cheeks. "It's all because of you," he said tenderly. "You brought everyone together. You would never stop fighting. And now I am here to stay, morning and night, until the end of my days."

The curse had truly been broken. Patrick had survived. Miranda had no words. Her tears were now of sheer joy. His loving green eyes soothed her. His touch healed her. And the couple shared a kiss that eclipsed all others before and since.

The story of Patrick Hyland McShane would be legend in Kilcrohane for generations to come. And the love he shared with Miranda Kelly would be felt in the Emerald Isle forever.

Read Next...

THE SHIFTY SERVANTS
By Maria Christine

Cooking, cleaning, saving kings...
It's all in a day's work.

For more information, visit
www.MariaChristineOnline.com